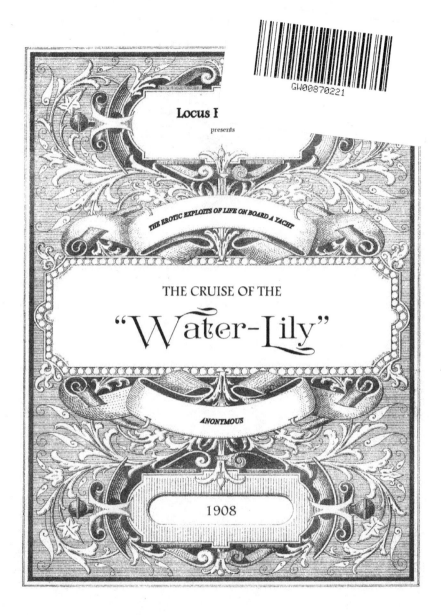

Locus E

presents

THE EROTIC EXPLOITS OF LIFE ON BOARD A YACHT

THE CRUISE OF THE

"Water-Lily"

ANONYMOUS

1908

LOCUS   ELM™

find more by typing

Locus_Elm_Press

at:

Amazon United Kingdom
Amazon United States of America
Amazon Germany
Amazon Netherlands
Amazon France
Amazon Spain
Amazon Canada
Amazon Australia
Amazon Brazil
Amazon Japan
Amazon Mexico
Amazon Italy
Amazon India

*

The Cruise of the "Water-Lily"

The Erotic Exploits of Life on Board a Yacht

by

Anonymous

written 1908

This paperback edition - Copyright: Locus Elm Press

Published: July 2016

TABLE OF CONTENTS

CHAPTER I...7
The Water-Lily

CHAPTER II...12
A Bouquet Of Flowers

CHAPTER III..19
An Adventure

CHAPTER IV..27
The Masked Ball On Board

CHAPTER V...41
Each One In His Turn

CHAPTER VI..45
The Refinements Of Captain Bullock

CHAPTER VII...51
An Agreeable Intermezzo

CHAPTER VIII..57
The Gentlemen Enjoy Themselves

CHAPTER IX..67
"L'appetit vient en mangeant"

CHAPTER X...72
The Final Plunge

CHAPTER I

*

The Water-Lily

The picturesque little town of Cannes, on the borders of the blue Mediterranean, is, as everyone knows, the winter rendezvous and port of meeting of a great number of pleasure yachts, mostly belonging to wealthy English owners, or to American millionaires, who come there to take part in the various regattas of the region, or else, after a brief sojourn on the coast of the Riviera, go for a cruise in Italian waters, sometimes landing to hunt boars and stags in Albania or Epirus.

At the time when the events occurred which form the subject of this narrative, some thirty yachts were at anchor in La Croisette bay, There were sea-going craft of all forms and dimensions, some flying under a princely or a ducal flag; others, though equally luxuriously equipped, contented themselves with sporting the pennant of some yacht club. Among these later, was one in particular, remarkable for its magnificence, its size, and the strangeness of its general appearance.

The arrival of the *Water-Lily* had excited the liveliest curiosity among the population and the winter residents, very numerous at that time of year. The yacht, extremely elegant in shape, was painted white all over, relieved by handsome gilt moulding along the line of bulwarks, and the side rails were also gilt. The smokestacks were of the same dazzling brilliant white hue, glittering in the sun. By a caprice of her owner, the *Water-Lily* was rigged so as not only to serve as a steam yacht, but also to be a fast sailing boat, and in fact it could outrace some of the smartest crack cutters. The sails were of a tender mauve tint, upon which stood out in relief large silver-coloured flowers affecting strange forms, something between those of the tulip and the lily.

The owner of this queer craft was certainly no ordinary man. No one had seen him as yet, his arrival having been announced for the next week only, at which time the *Water-Lily* was to weigh anchor, bound for a cruise along the coast of Turkish Epirus.

Lord Reginald Seacombe, the proprietor of the yacht, had the reputation of being a thoroughly eccentric nobleman. He had strange fancies, and some people even dared to pretend that he had something wrong in the cerebral regions. His father, who had amassed a large fortune by brewing stout and pale ale, had died leaving a very respectable number of millions, which the son was doing his best to get rid of with the utmost placidity of mind. He at times committed the greatest follies, and in the fashionable clubs he frequented, it was almost proverbial to say, "prodigal as Reggie Seacombe".

Public rumour had it that the excessively rich Englishman was trying to copy in all and everything the late King of Bavaria, who met with so tragic a death in the waters of the Lake of Starnberg. Lord Seacombe loved fantastical castles, wild drives in the middle of the night in his motor-car, or for a change, in a fairy coach on lonely mountains, when the vehicle, drawn by fiery horses, would be resplendent with electric lamps.

Although difficult to verify, the gossiping whispers bear some semblance of reality as far as his yacht went. If its exterior arrangements, it was a positive masterpiece of originality.

The author of this narrative, accompanying as secretary Count X..., who had been invited by Lord Seacombe to join him in his cruise in Turkish waters, was in a situation to be able to judge, and in the interest of the readers of this little story, he has collected his slightest souvenirs to draw a faithful a picture as possible of the interior arrangements of the *Water-Lily*.

The yacht was about 3,000 tons burden; consequently, it was of very respectable dimensions, and as a ship, could offer its own all the comfort that could be desired.

The cabins, fifty in number, were fitted up with the utmost luxury. All imaginable refinements were concentrated within them. They were spacious and nicely furnished. Besides the cabins, the yacht contained a vast saloon, a spacious dining cabin, and an immense bathroom, without counting several dressing and bath-rooms for the private use of the guests.

The saloon and dining-room presented nothing particular beyond the extreme luxury of their arrangement and the audacious richness of their decoration.

The same could not be said of the large bathing hall. This room was about eighteen yards long, and six in width. It was entirely paved, and the walls were lined with slabs of white and red-veined marble, the ceiling being covered in the same way. Here and there were placed large beveled Venice mirrors; all around the place were low Turkish divans and Persian rugs, whilst the corners were occupied by exotic plants and flowering shrubs in profusion. In the centre of the hall was a vast swimming bath lined with white marble, and having silver taps to supply alternately warm and cold water. In the middle was a fountain, worked by a small and ingenious electric motor, and in every corner were aquatic plants placed behind trellis-work so as to be safe from the hot water.

A number of canaries, goldfinches and other birds of gorgeous plumage flew at liberty within the hall which was arranged in quite idyllic fashion, creating the illusion of an antique garden with its piscina and busts of white marble.

Lord Reginald and his friends used to give themselves up to joyous sports in this palatial bathing saloon, such as wrestling in the water, and other sorts of games. The host was himself an intrepid swimmer.

He often brought some ladies with this friends and they then all took sea baths together, en petit comite on board the yacht itself. I was told that they sometimes amused themselves in very free fashion on these occasions of mixed bathing. But this was merely a passing murmur of scandal that I was not in a position to verify until later.

The saloon was in Oriental style. Everywhere about were low divans, cushions, hangings and carpets in profusion. The entire effect was soft, intimate, reposeful, and highly—nay, sensually—suggestive.

The crew of the yacht was composed of some forty picked men, and the noble owner, who held a master's certificate, took command himself. He had chosen as first mate one of his personal friends, a retired officer of the United States' Navy.

I was told that this officer had been forced to tender his resignation as a result of certain conduct not altogether laudable. He had abducted a captain's daughter, with whom he had cohabited for some months, afterwards abandoning her. These details, by the way, are scarcely superfluous, for they may ultimately explain certain things otherwise obscure.

The *Water-Lily*, it may be seen, was a pleasure yacht unique of its kind, so to say, well arranged to serve the most extravagant whims of its eccentric owner and of a company of joyous blasé rakes, seeking for the greatest refinements in their voluptuous pleasures.

Count X..., my master, was not behindhand in this respect. He was surprisingly apt in all that pertained to lustful delight and its derivations.

I had been informed that we should start with the owner of the yacht and that I had to hold myself in readiness, for the Count had some literary pretentions, although he was not even capable of inditing his amorous missives himself.

He always charged me to write them in his stead. This often enabled me to profit by his good fortunes — at his expense, of course. He particularly wished me to accompany him in order to write a narration of the cruise which he purposed publishing on his return.

We shall see later how, by force of circumstances, he was unable to execute this project.

A few days before the arrival of Lord Reginald, a great quantity of provisions and ammunition was brought on board. I happened to be on deck at that moment, having been busy seeing that the cabin of Count X..., was properly-arranged. He liked his ease and comfort, and for that trusted rather to his valet, to do my best to render his stay on board as agreeable as possible.

This enormous cargo was not without causing me some surprise. I knew that the number of persons invited was about twenty, which together with the crew, petty officers, engineers, stokers, coal trimmers, cooks, stewards, etc. would form a total muster of seventy-five at least. But, according to my calculations, the amount of food-stuffs embarked would have been sufficient for a cruise to the South Pole without having to put in anywhere, and yet I knew that the yacht was to call at Naples and Messina.

Busy as I was, however, and not particularly inquisitive by nature, I did not attach much, importance to the victualling I had made until the day when I was informed of the advent of Lord Seacombe, at the same time that Count X... gave me instructions for preparing to embark on the following day.

CHAPTER II

*

A Bouquet Of Flowers

Lord Reginald had arrived and all his guests with him. On the male side, they numbered seven, which together with the owner and Count X... made up nine sons of Adam.

The fair sex was represented by eight lady passengers, who assembled together, formed the most graceful bouquet of natural flowers that can be imagined. Their beauty and grace vied with the freshness of their youth and I could not help admitting that the gentlemen had shown no bad taste at all, and that in bringing each of profound knowledge of anthropology as well as of plastic art. My master was the only real bachelor in the company.

A single glance, however, showed that among all these fair dames there was not one who could lay claim to legitimate royalty. They were all of them queens, queens of beauty, but morganatic!

I shall not waste any time in presenting here the portraits of Lord Reginald's male friends. Men, when they belong to the "Upper Ten", and more especially to the clan of high livers, dudes, and tip-top swells, all resemble one another, or pretty nearly so: supreme elegance, chic pushed to the limits of extravagance, and clothes of the same cut or thereabouts, made by fashionable tailors.

But on the side of the ladies there was ample matter for observation, and, on my word, had I been charged with the mission of awarding the apple to the loveliest of the eight, I should certainly have been far more embarrassed than Paris himself.

I will now endeavour to paint as faithfully as possible the portraits of the pretty female passengers, whom these gentlemen had invited to accompany them on this cruise, which is likely to become in the full meaning of the word — a voyage to Cythcrea, for as in all probability we may go as far as Smyrna, that will oblige us to double the cape, at the point of which is perched, stretching far out in the sea, the island sacred to Venus and to love.

My descriptions is, of course, made from the notes recorded by me afterwards, and from conversations that I chanced to overhear.

First of all, I must notice that three of these dames belonged to the demi-monde. They were elegant high priestesses of Eros, and they had gained a preponderating grade in the battalion of Venus. There were also two actresses well known to the public of the principal Parisian theatres. These latter were not altogether of the "half-world", but they were not too inaccessible to that always victorious argument which presents itself under the form of new crisp banknotes.

The three other female guests were, one of them, a seamstress escaped from the workshop of a great dressmaking establishment of the Rue de la Paix, where on account of her sculptural charms, she had been employed as mannequin or "tryer-on". She had let herself be ensnared by a not over serious lover who, one day, had left her in the lurch when he had enough of her, leaving her nothing but the choice of going back to legitimate work, or of launching out into gay life.—After short hesitation and a very brief return to the workshop, she cast herself in the arms of the first admirer she met and with whom she led the life of true love and felt no remorse, as everything worked smoothly until the day I saw her on board the *Water-Lily*. The two others were still rather unfledged. They had listened to the suggestions of their friend and had flung decorum to the winds. — The sweetheart of the young dressmaker has asked her if she could not bring along with her five or six of her friends. Not withstanding all her efforts to oblige, she had only been able to engage these two — real jewels, it is true — but who wanted nothing better than to exchange the life of the workshop for the enjoyments with which the temptress had dazzled their eyes. As I shall have occasion to insist upon later, they were still in possession of their capital — which is polite French for "maidenhead". They had not yet seen the "wolf in the fold" but were expecting him, not without a certain amount of anxiety and fear at the approach of the moment when they would have to take "the fatal jump".

The eldest of the lady guests, she who exhibited the most luxurious frocks, was known in all the gayest resorts of pleasure— seeking Paris by the name of Liane de Vibrecoeur. She was altogether of most seductive appearance. Fair as the ripening corn; a magnificent head of hair, all in delicious curly disorder, which served admirably to set off perfect features, with large blue eyes shadowed by long, languishing lashes; her nose was small and nervous; her mouth of suggestive shape, and she had very small, pearly ears. She resembled one of those charming dolls that are to be seen in the windows of the richest toyshops, where babies spoilt by fortune find their most sumptuous playthings.

Liane de Vibrecoeur, by a well-studied and very particular arrangement of her dress, knew how to set off all the beauty of her form, which had caused it to be said of her, even by her rivals, that she was built to model.

Although barely five and twenty years of age, she had already devoured two fortunes, and was beginning to nibble at that of her third protector, who accompanied her on board, Count Oscar Popolsky, a rich nobleman from Warsaw. This latter gentleman, with the exception of Count X... was the only male guest on board who was not English or American.

Her friend, Geo Montauciel, had the reputation of being the wildest little madcap in Cupid's regiment. She was twenty-two years old, and possessed all the charm and beauty of blooming youth. Well built; a delicious bust and voluptuous hips, she could pass for being extremely dangerous. Ardent and impassioned in the highest degree, she gave no respite to her lovers, and the sturdy gentleman who kept her, a robust Welsh squire, had, it appears, as much as he could well do to calm the amorous temperament of the lovely lass who had managed to bring his weight down by seven pounds within a fortnight.

The third light o'love invited was the perfect type of the languishing young Woman, who finds in her indifference, in her affectation of ennui, the force to charm and captivate men. She was of dark complexion, distinguished looking, very slender in the waist, her breasts well formed, and with delicate hands and feet. There was in her features I know not what of attractive sympathetic allurement, and on her sensual lips there always seemed to lover some loving words.

Like Geo Montauciel, she also was just twenty-two years old, and she answered to the graceful name of Stella Carina — the beloved star.

The two actresses, who took part in our excursion, formed between them a perfect contrast. The one, tall, slender and fair, of that shade of blonde which reminds one of chemically prepared tresses, was indifference personified. Her features were perfectly regular; her bust very long; her figure willowy, and her head smilingly swaying on a firm and tempting neck. In all her gestures, in her walk and even in her speech, could be noticed affected lassitude and boredom. But, after all, she was a real charmer, perfectly able to arouse the most violent and burning desires in men. She was known in the artistic world by the name of Blanche de Noirmont. Her age was from twenty-three to twenty-four years.

Esther Hazy, her companion, differed totally from pretty Blanche de Noirmont. They were both about the same age, but, as much as Blanche was languishing and apathetic, so much did Esther giro proof of vivacity, warmth and outbursts of temper. She was like quicksilver. Small in stature, well proportioned in every way, her skin swarthy like that of an Andalusian girl, with a wild shock of black hair; she was the perfect type of the woman of the South, with hot blood seething in her veins. Her large dark eyes shot flashes of lightning as she opened her mouth to speak as rapidly as a mill-wheel when the river runs high. She was heart and soul a "glee maiden" ever ready for amorous sport, thinking of naught but love and pleasure, exclaiming: "After me — the deluge!"

Esther had found a good English fellow who spent his money for her without counting and gave way to all her whims and fancies.

The young wench who, from the show-room at the Rue de la Paix, where she had been a mannequin, had thought it more practical, and above all more lucrative, to transfer her activity elsewhere, had also adopted a nom de guerre. She took to herself that of Odette Myosotis. She had been so often assured that her eyes reflected a beam from the azure of heaven and that their brightness could never be forgotten, for her not to jump at the opportunity of taking possession of a name more graceful than her own. The title she had adopted contained a motto: "Forget me not!" And no doubt the artful jade possessed all requisite qualities enabling her never to be forgotten.

She was built like a goddess of antiquity; her sculptural form set off by a princesse dress which suited her to perfection, and added to her appearance something captivating which made a tremor of lust pass through the veins of men. Her gentlemen friend used to call her the "Venus of Milo". She was certainly a handsome woman from head to foot, and her special charm was her head of hair which she committed the great error of transforming into a very golden blonde hue. She used to take pleasure in letting down her tresses and allowing those yellow silky folds to float at the mercy of the breeze, when some amber locks would reach down to her heels.

It was therefore not surprising that handsome Odette Myosotis should have rapidly made her way, and was now kept in grand style by a wealthy Englishman, who did things in princely fashion, as only Englishmen know how to, scattering gold with unflinching calmness for the sake of the young woman who had at least the virtue of showing him some signs of gratitude.

Renee Danglars, one of Odette's little friends, was just as sufficiently depraved as apprentice Parisian workgirl who aspires to a more brilliant destiny needs to be. She was a pretty as possible and carried the grace of her nineteen summers triumphantly about Paris. She was gay, beaming, and eager for sensuous emotions and adventures of all kinds. Already she could boast of having had two miniature love intrigues, but at the critical moment she always managed to stop the train in time. ' The locomotive had been able to reach to the entrance of the tunnel, without ever having succeeded in penetrating. But now she was decided to go the whole hog.

She was well developed for her age, and was not badly built, although rather weak in the chest. That slight defect Was compensated by the beauty of her legs and thighs which were altogether tempting. She had besides that particular charm which distinguishes the prime of youth. She was just a trifle awkward, although she did all she possibly could to appear wide-awake and roguish.

But that suited her so well! With her frizzly wealth of fair hair and big curls; her fresh pretty face and pert little expression, she appeared like some tasty, luscious fruit, barely ripe enough, into which one would like to bite as soon as the eyes perceive it.

Micheline Darcourt was only seventeen years old. Seventeen — sweet seventeen! The age of love's young dream and ideal joy.

But in the corrupting atmosphere of the workroom, she had lost that real innocence which constitutes young virgin's charm. Micheline was still physically a maid. Her body was intact, but her soul was no longer immaculate, or as Balzac, says, Vierge de corps, chaste, non! In fact, she had arrived at that point when the most trifling event might decide the fate of the damsel.

She was not wonderfully handsome, but she was gloriously, unknowingly handsome. Seductive, sensually, attractive, she had that silly kind of beauty which requires to be strongly seasoned and roused by stimulants in order to be fully appreciated. Micheline had hesitated before thus surrendering herself. The promises of fine dresses, jewels, and pleasures innumerable, with the prospect of and idle life, had caused her to make up her mind, and she followed along the carpeted gangway.

Nevertheless, Micheline was not without some apprehensions. She looked forward with a certain amount of terror to the moment when" something would be done to her". And she was not in the least reassured, for she was fearful of the slightest pain. The prick of a pin would make her jump again, and in spite of the enjoyments and pleasures had out in perspective, she trembled at the idea of the first shock, for she knew that it was not without being accompanied by cries and gnashing of teeth. Odette raised her courage as well she could by persuasive means, but Micheline, under a merry and frivolous exterior, dissimulated her secret terrors, and it was easy to see that if she had been able to do so, she would have backed out. It was too late.

She had embarked and well embarked in this undertakings and must go through with it to the end.

Such was the company assembled on board the *Water-Lily*, when that stately vessel got up steam to start upon its cruise.

CHAPTER III

*

An Adventure

Two days after our departure from Cannes. Lord Seacombe gave me a first proof of his originality by having the yacht's course altered and steering for Nice where we put in the next day.

The Carnival was in full swing. The streets were thronged with maskers and the festival was at its highest point of brilliancy and fun.

All the company went on shore and took part in the amusements. I was informed by my employer that it had been unanimously agreed to—get up a masked ball on board the *Water-Lily*, but as we had no fancy costumes with us, we had turned back to Nice to get some. But here a difficulty arose. The dresses obtainable in that town were not to the taste of Lord Reginald who particularly objected that they were not sufficiently suggestive.

While joking, at supper he had promised a prize of one thousand pounds sterling to that one among the ladies who should be declared to be the best dressed by a vote of the gentlemen assembled as jury to decide to whom should be awarded the palm as the most ingeniously and tastefully disguised.

It is needless to say that furnished all these of Lord Seacombe had furnished all these dames with unlimited credit at the establishment of the Opera costumier and the other principal dressmakers of the Queen of the Mediterranean.

This caprice permitted us to remain six days on the coast of the Riviera.

All the ladies had set to worth on their costumes in the greatest secrecy and it was impossible; even by a few very slight indiscretions to learn what surprise they reserved to us for the projected fancy dress ball.

Our stay at Nice had permitted Count X... to amuse himself in his peculiar way. As he belonged to that part of the country, he met several friends and went to flirt with the dark-haired beauties of the neighbourhood, and I had the advantage of accompanying him in all his excursions. Thus it was that a singular adventure occurred to us on the second day after our arrival.

The Count and I were rambling about, without any fixed purpose, he gazing at the stars, I, casting right and left inquisitive looks to see if anything worthy of attention should occur, when, all at once at the corner of a quiet side street, I noticed a woman, evidently in humble circumstances, strangely decked out in all sorts of antiquated finery, like a dealer in second-hand female attire on the spree. She smiled at me.

By her side was a young girl of about sixteen years of age, also curiously dressed, but of most fascinating beauty. She was fair, of such a blonde as I had never seen, but her face, purely oval, rather long, was lit up by two large black eyes, all humid and languishing, and their glance went straight to my heart.

"Oh, the lovely girl!" I exclaimed, in spite of myself. The Count turned round, and — genuine connoisseur that he was — recognised that I had not been mistaken. He was gifted with that special talent which enables a man to undress a woman at a glance and to discover beneath her rags all the perfection as well as the imperfections of her person.

He went on a few paces with me and then said!

"That old woman seems like a procuress. I must leave you now. Try and find out what she w. I give you carte-blanche if there is anything to be done, but in any case, try not to get in a mess. Don't compromise the situation. The little minx is certainly worthy of being looked after."

And making a significant sign of discreet understanding, the Count then left me.

I turned back again, meeting the couple, and the old woman addressed to me the same inviting smile as before.

I did not know exactly what to do so as to make no blunder, which might after all be possible. I therefore asked the old lady to direct me to a distant quarter.

She was not the dupe of my stratagem, and winking, said:

"Come along with me! I will show her to you!"

This was said in patois, half French and half Piedmontese. She took me on one side, while the lovely girl remained alone at the corner of the street like a virgin Corregio in a niche.

"What do you think of her — the little girl, I mean, eh?" She went straight to the point.

"Admirable, delicious!" I answered, seeing that I had to do with an Italian woman, and knowing how prone are Italians to exaggerate.

"Well, how much will you give to enjoy her?"

I remained for a moment somewhat astounded, for I could not suppose the business would go off so quickly. The old woman did not beat about the bush. Without the least shame, she offered her living merchandise.

As matters were so far simplified, I was no longer obliged to observe any reserve. So I asked the old matron:

"What sum of money do you want, and how is it with your little one?"

The old woman explained to me that the young beauty was a niece of hers, who had come that day from Asti, in Piedmont, and who would be very gentle—very obedient. The elderly dealer in human flesh did not precisely affirm that the lass's virginity had been preserved with the greatest care so as to be sold all the more dearly in France, but I could make that much out clearly enough from what the old hag said to me.

It was, however, necessary not to be in too great a hurry and keep up appearances. I therefore informed her, that my master was an amateur painter seeking for a model; adding also that he worked a great deal from the nude, and that he consequently required models who were not likely to play the demure with him. His chosen model should be prepared to sit for "the altogether", and as my master travelled a good deal, she would as my master travelled a good deal, she would have to consent to travel also and to be absent sometimes for two or three weeks running.

"That makes no matter! The pichina will go wherever she may be required to go, so long as payment is made in advance."

"And how much will that be?" I ventured to enquire.

"Twenty francs a day for the first month, and fifteen francs a day for the next three months, always paid in advance."

As I appeared to reflect, the old humbug hastened to add:

"You know, she'll do whatever you like. She'll be your maid of all worth — of all work, ha! ha!

The procuress was cynically taking steps to open my mind and I could no longer have any doubts. I gave no answer but seemed reflecting again.

Seeing that I was hesitating, the old dame drew me on one side, and said to me in her jargon:

"If you wish to have proof that she is still a virgin, I will get a certificate from a medical man and you can choose him yourself."

"Useless! useless!" I retort. "It is not that. I am seeking for a model for my employer — a model, you understand, and nothing more!"

"I understand", answered the old woman, with a wink and a sufficiently suggestive smile.

"In any case, I must go and speak with him had but little confidence in that slip of paper. On the subject", I continued, in order to put an end to the conversation which inspired me with disgust, for I was quite convinced that I was negotiating with a mother selling her own daughter.

I requested the venerable harridan to wait a moment for me at the place where she stood, and to excuse me for not taking her to a cafe from fear of compromising the young girl.

She promised to wait for me, so I returned to the Count and explained matters to him. I was careful, however, I admit to my shame, to slightly abuse the confidence he reposed in me, by informing him that I must take back an answer the same evening and that the next day the girl would be at his disposal.

Without hesitation, the Count handed me a cheque for six hundred francs, telling me to do the best I could, to take the necessary precautions and to bring him the girl the next day on board the yacht. Following his advice, I did not let her out of my sight.

After having rejoined the old woman and the little Madonna at the place where they were still waiting for me, I took them to a small retired cafe where I handed the cheque to the matron. But she therefore had to call a fiacre, and in it we all three proceeded to my hotel, where the cheque was at once cashed. This put the old lady in good humour and as it was I who had paid the money, she considered me as the buyer, and gave the little fairy all the necessary instructions. On the way, I bought the adorable child a little ring, which made her jump with joy.

It stands to reason that the instructions given by the old woman to the girl were only generalities, without entering into details. She was t" obey me in everything!

That was already a good deal! I do not insist upon the scene of the adieux. They were very tender. The little one cried — the old one blubbered, and I was well-nigh shedding tears, if only to join in chorus. I then led the girl away with me.

I took her first to a cafe, and offered her some refreshment, and afterwards to a restaurant where we had supper, whilst the waiter, instructed by me, went to engage a double-bedded room in a neighbouring hotel.

I had my plan — and after all, charity begins at home!

The girl was very docile. Was it ingenuousness or vice? I cannot say. The fact is she followed me without hesitating. I explained to her that I was obliged to make her pass for my sister, that she would have to sleep in the same room with me, but in her own separate bed.

She made no objection and all went on without any hitch, until we came into the bedroom.

It was time for us now to go to bed, and the poor lass began to show the first signs of hesitation.

She stood there, without making a movement, like a statue, and not daring to undress.

"Come, Giovanina", I said — her name was Giovanina Metelli. "Come, don't be foolish. What will you do when you will be asked to sit as model?"

"All naked?" she asked in consternation.

"Certainly! Quite naked!"

She looked me straight in the face and shrugging her shoulders with an air of incredulity, she added:

"Is that true — the honest truth?"

I assured her once more that it was so.

She then uttered a sigh and, no doubt accustomed to passive obedience, murmured in Italian:

"Since it must be!"

And she began to undress. I wanted to help her, but she would not permit it, pushing me gently away.

I then seated myself on the edge of my bed and quietly prepared to contemplate the enticing spectacle that I expected.

In the meanwhile, she had taken off her bodice, and her arms bare, her glorious breasts set off by a chemise, perfectly white though of coarse material, she stopped, and looking at me, suddenly said:

"But you also—are you not going to take your things off?"

I may be mistaken, but I seemed to me as if I could discern in the eyes of the lovely child that unseemly curiosity to which give birth the first desires of the ripe virgin.

Without saying a word, I started undressing in my turn, and the damsel continued also to divest herself of her clothing, revealing to me little by little all her secret charms. When we were both of us half nude, I, in my shirt, and she in her chemise, one in front of the other, we stopped, looking at each other, asking, as it were:

"Well, and what next?"

I could not withstand the temptation to kiss the charming creature, and I did it deliberately without her opposing the least resistance.

She then begged of me to get into bed, which I did at once, so much was I disconcerted. She then slipped between her sheets, and I blew out the light. But I could not sleep and I soon became aware that Giovanina also had not closed her eyes.

Then, being no longer able to resist, I lit the candle again, boldly got out of my bed, and approached that of the beautiful girl.

"What do you want?" she asked with exquisite simplicity. Without long fishing about for a pretext, I replied:

"I feel cold. I think we should be better two together. Be good enough to make a little room for me."

"But how can you think of such a thing?" she objected. "A man in bed with me?"

"Oh, that does not matter! " I replied. "You will sooner or later have to sleep with a man."

"Yes, but that will be my husband!" was her reply.

Without adding a word, I lifted up the bedclothes, and slipped into the bed, taking good care to avoid touching her.

At the end of a moment, a first involuntary rub of my knee against her thigh was inevitable.

A sort of electric shock ensued, and then there was a closer approach. Little by little, in spite of some slight resistance on her part, I held her in my arms.

Seeing, now, that for me the game was almost won, I began to kiss and embrace her. She let me continue without protesting in the least, but also without returning me a single touch of her lips. She was altogether passive. I became emboldened, and caressed her full throat, and her little bubbles, quite firm, solid as marble. I kissed her soft belly and my hand strayed as far as her pussy. She had progressively undergone these different sensations without making any opposition, and I thought that I could even perceive that she found a certain pleasure in this game — evidently new to her. I succeeded in making her enjoy by means of my finger, and then for the first time she went so far as to press her mouth to my moustache. She had become like a toy in my arms. I was burning with the desire of possessing her and, seeing that she did not quite comprehend the situation, I managed at last to make her understand that what I wanted was something more than those little games which she seemed to think was all there was to be done. She made some timid protests, but as, in virtue of my temporary power, I reminded her of the words of her aunt according to which she was to obey me in everything, she gave way with docility.

"What am I to do?" she asked.

"I will show you", I said.

Stretching her out on the bed, I made her open her thighs. She made no resistance. But when I laid myself atop of her, and placed in her little hand my big tool, as stiff as a rod of iron, she became afraid.

"Put it inside your body", said I to her. "Show him the road!"

She could not make up her mind to that, and had a movement of revolt. I was too randy not to go ahead. With one brisk gesture, I seized her in my arms, and sought to introduce my member into her slit. I partly succeeded, but perhaps I had undertaken the job awkwardly, for she began to cry and to hit me feebly in the ribs, calling out that I was "brutal".

"Well then, let me do it to you gently," said I.

After a short struggle, she gave in, and, half fainting, all shaken with voluptuous tremors, she for the first time received the essential baptism, the only one that gives tangible fruits — sometimes, but not always.

She remained in a partial swoon for about half an hour. I contemplated her tranquilly, with the pride of a cock who has just been treading a hen without defence — but perchance none too unwilling after all!

The sheets were covered in blood. I cared not.

I wiped the ruby fluid from the linen, from my prick, and from my victim's thighs, and my eyes, dilated with desire, never ceased staring at her loveliness.

It was some time before she recovered her full consciousness, and then her first gesture was to lay feverishly hold of my weapon. She instinctively guided it to her nest of love. I required no other invitation. I possessed her. I took and rogered her again and again until the morning — and I did the same the next day, having found a pretext for making the Count wait.

But when I conducted Giovanina Metelli, the all lovely and adorable Piedmontese lassie, to the Count, her rightful owner, for was he not her purchaser? — she was no longer a virgin. Furthermore, I had made her believe that all sorts of annoying troubles would be her lot if she continued protesting her innocence. I was not wrong in acting thus, for up to the present day the beautiful girl is still mine, and I know pertinently that she has never been possessed by anyone else. I took my precautions far too well.

CHAPTER IV

*

The Masked Ball On Board

When I conducted Giovanina to the Count and after I had acquainted him with the pretended avowal of the young girl relating to the loss of her virginity some short time previously, he appeared greatly annoyed and disappointed. But as he was a queer customer in his way, all he said was:

"So much the worse for me, but all the better for you. I give her up to you. You may amuse yourself with the damsel as long as you like, but first of all I wish to realise a project I have conceived, and which I trust will be fully successful."

I could not for the moment learn any more on the subject, but as I wished for nothing better than to keep the girl for myself, I purchased for her a few necessary toilet articles, and had her dressed up at my expense. When she was nicely decked out from head to foot, she really looked extremely well, being very pretty, so much so that I dreaded for a moment that my master, the Count, might change his mind and take her from me again.

Fortunately such was not the case and I was able to enjoy my conquest in perfect peace.

The Count, however, had advised me to dissimulate as much

possible the presence of Giovanina on board, and excepting two or three persons who had been let into the secret, none of Lord Seacombe's guests, nor even his lordship himself, had the slightest inkling of the truth.

We had weighed anchor, and the following evening, in splendid weather and with a smooth sea, in sight of the Italian coast, off Civita Vecchia, the bal masque was given at last.

All the ladies had made their preparations in the closed secrecy; nothing of their plans had been divulged and we were justified in expecting some dainty surprises.

The Count had revealed his plan to me, and had charged me to induce little Giovanina to wear the disguise he had invented for her, I had to put forward all my powers of persuasion, for the lovely lassie had become really attached to me. But when I explained that her assistance was required so as to get up a scene that the Count intended to paint, she finally consented to do all he required.

The grand saloon was magnificently decorated with tropical plants, garlands of flowers and Japanese lanterns. The aspect was fairy-like.

I will not enter into useless details. Let it suffice for me to say that the gentlemen, in full evening dress, were assembled at one end of the saloon, where I had also been admitted to act the part of "introducer of the masqueraders," when the grand electric orchestration, which the foresight of Lord Reginald had not omitted to provide, began to resound.

He had merely to press a button and the magnificent organ, built to reproduce the seventy-two instruments of a full band, started playing as introduction, a selection from "Cavalttera Rusticana". This was resplendent with local colour in Italian waters, within sight of the coast where the maestro Mascagni had first seen the light.

Liane de Vibrecoeur — noblesse oblige — was the first to make her entry. She had chosen an entirely mythological disguise, being dressed to represent Ceres, the harvest goddess, and the costume suited her to perfection. Lightly clad in a very thin tunic of natural silk, artistically draped, and fastened at the waist by a girdle of wild poppies, her richly developed breasts, luscious as ripe fruit, emerged from the drapery fixed to her shoulders by a bunch of golden wheat-ears. Her blonde tresses were appropriately adorned with cornflowers, poppies and ears of corn, and her slim but nervous legs were also to be viewed — just enough, but not too much of them — encased in flesh-colour tights.

A murmur of applause welcomed the apparition of Liane de Vibrecoeur, who took her seat by the side of her lord and master, and I, in the execution of my functions, proceeded to introduce the second siren in fancy dress.

This was Renee Danglars, in all the glory of her beauty. Artless as she was, and wishing to give a racy touch to the entertainment, she appeared in the garb of a merveilleuse of the days of the Directoire.

Nothing was wanting in the details. She had always the same adorable little face, and in her clever disguise, had managed to enhance all the perfections with which Nature had adorned her.

Vain of the beauty of her breasts which stood out stiffly proud in her corsage, cut outrageously low, she had, in conformity with the fashion of the period, allowed the white flesh of her firm thighs to show through the side of her gown, slit from hip to ankle. She had taken the precaution not to put on fleshings, and advanced dressed all in black satin, trimmed with rose-coloured ribbons and white lace. She had great taste and knew how to show off her bodily charms to advantage. Her brilliantly white and velvety skin contrasted agreeably with the sable hue of her dress. She was sensuously suggestive in the highest degree. But she had not yet altogether the art of pleasing, or of being alluring, and although she was as desirable as possible, she had not the same success as her competitor, Liane de Vibrecoeur; notwithstanding, Renee was a lovely creature.

Her friend, Micheline, who had asked to follow immediately after her, although awkward and now wanted to play the part of a bold beauty.

She had chosen as her costume Diana going to the bath. We were altogether steeped in mythology that night.

As I said before, she was only seventeen and had found out that in the midst of such a galaxy of beauty, it was necessary for her to get on audaciously full steam ahead.

For this occasion, she had adopted a most primitive costume. Her legs, very well shaped, and innocent of fleshings, were immodestly exposed to the gaze of all. The naughty lass had confidence in herself, knowing admirably how to draw attention to her well-made, plump carves, destined to excite the senses.

She had intentionally left exposed her maiden breasts, already splendidly developed and palpitating with emotion, and they stood out erect and rigid as if inviting caresses. She showed the upper part of her virginal belly, between two half-open folds of her loosely flowing, scanty dress, very simple in cut, by the way, and of snow-white mousseline de soie, with, for sole trimming, a girdle of gold. In her hair she carried a crescent incrusted with imitation diamonds.

The artless child scarcely anticipated the sensation she would create, and she involuntarily obtained most extraordinary success. In the timid exhibition of some small portion of her anatomy, she had unwittingly been able to exercise that talent which renders the get-up of a woman's dress eminently provoking.

She found her reward in a passionate embrace from her lover who, in point of fact, was such as yet only platonically, and that evening, I thought I could read in her eyes that the decisive moment had arrived.

In short, little Micheline Darcourt was simply delicious.

Cleo Montauciel had selected a disguise well in keeping with her disposition. She represented Satan, in very close-fitting black silk tights, spangled with innumerable little silver stars. Thus was her fascinating shape advantageously defined. By a sort of refinement of coquetry, she had carefully avoided exhibiting the least scrap of naked flesh, but she was none the less a sorceress with her lascivious swaying hips. She had tolerable success.

Esther Hazy, who came next, had not the talent to please more than quite indifferently. She had taken the part of a nymph, which did not suit her far too vivacious and joyous nature. She had evidently aimed at exciting the senses, but had only succeeded in being commonplace. She made a favourable impression, her costume being rich, but altogether she was nothing extraordinary.

It was now the turn of Stella Carina. With exquisite taste, she had hit upon a disguise which without being overpoweringly original, had still the merit of being well chosen, and neatly carried out. She appeared as a flower-girl.

Perched saucily upon her small head was a Leghorn straw bat, garnished with bunches of grapes and wild flowers. She wore a rose-coloured velvet bodice, liberally low-necked, so as to allow the nipples of her rosy, budding breasts to be just perceptible, like strawberries barely ripe. Very short sleeves gave passage to her full, rounded, tempting arms, terminated by slender wrists and very delicate, soft, white hands. A very short skirt allowed her admirably moulded legs to be seen up to the knees and even higher, as far as the beginning of the thighs, encased in tight blue silk stockings, maintained without a wrinkle by black silk garters garnished with shells and artificial violets. Her calves were worthy of being kissed, and her feet — real gems — were fitted into tiny shoes of a peach-blossom tint.

In fact, taken all together, Stella Carina was a treasure of grace, voluptuous beauty, and promise of enjoyment. In my opinion, she was the handsomest woman we had yet seen, and deserved the prize, for the elegance of her costume and the undefinable charm of her person.

Blanche de Noirmont, the great actress, had taken a costume from her stock theatrical wardrobe. She appeared under the aspect of a genuine Valkyrie, without modesty, and not caring to hide from the eyes of mortals the charms bestowed upon her by the Gods. But she did not display enough energy in her bearing, and despite her armour, was not sufficiently imperious, so that notwithstanding the splendid effect she produced, her disguise could not obtain the unanimous suffrages of the gentlemen spectators.

Only Odette Myosotis now remained. Sure of the effect she expected to produce, she advanced gravely, representing Juno, the goddess of goddesses with her luxuriant her dyed red. Her bare neck and throat, her exciting hips, and her heaving breasts emerged from a confused mass of rose-coloured gauze and white ribbons. Her legs were bare. She was delicious, intoxicating, and the glimpse of her sculptural charms, which were mere than divined as they peeped through her floating drapery, could not fail to arouse strong sensuality in a manly breast.

There was once more a long buzz of admiration on her entrance, and the other women bit their carmine lips in spiteful jealousy.

Sure of her triumph. Odette bowed graciously before the assembled company and then seated herself by her lover's side.

It was about to be decided to whom should be awarded the prize offered by Lord Seacombe, when Gaunt X... rose from his seat.

"Begging your pardon, gentlemen", he said, "you have each of you introduced your candidate. Permit me in my turn to present mine."

And as everybody began to exchange looks of the utmost amazement, the Count made a sign to me, upon which I went towards the door. But before leaving the saloon, I bowed to the company and announced very simply:

"Venus rising from the sea!"

I then went to fetch Giovanina. The Count had caused a large artificial shell to be made which moved upon concealed wheels. Outside the doorway, the young girl mounted on the gigantic sea shell, which I began pushing before me into the saloon.

She made stark naked, draped only in her long tresses of Venetian blonde hair; a chaste smile on her lips, and totally unconscious of the magical effect she was producing on the entire company.

Her thighs, chastely pressed together, just permitted the vision of a few stray wanton hairs shading the sanctuary of love.

Her legs, admirably modelled, with firm calves, and her fair skin showed gloriously against the dark background. Her young breasts, swollen with emotion, jutted out hard and firm, seeming to invite the touch of libertine hands, while her trembling lips were also begging for love's kisses.

She was radiant and comely, as lovely as a star fallen from the realms of paradise.

By unanimous consent, the men, without having to consult each other, awarded her the palm. The prize was hers. Lord Seacombe took beautiful Giovanina in his arms and kissed her with rather more lengthy warmth than I exactly cared for. She passed thus from hand to hand, kissed and caressed by all the eager males, finally landing at my side, in tears, troubled exceedingly, and blushing like a virgin just escaped from a convent.

Among the ladies present there was a general feeling of indignation. They smelt a rival, and a sharp discussion having ensued, the Count took me on one side, and begged me to lead Giovanina back again to her cabin.

I wished for nothing better, for I was beginning to grow jealous in spite of myself. So I soon conducted my little Italian beauty to my berth, where I told her to remain while I returned to the ball, to see what was going on.

The orchestration was playing that lively waltz, Strauss's "Blue Danube", and to its strains, a number of the dancing with animation. Champagne was flowing like water, and in a very short time the general jollity rose to an extraordinarily high pitch.

Liane de Vibrecoeur, Cleo Montauciel and Stella Carina, already slightly tipsy, had allowed themselves to be carried away by the effects of the sparkling wine, and were whirling in a high-kicking, indecent can-can of the wildest description. Blanche de Noirmont and Esther Hazy, following in their capering steps, under the inspiriting influence of several foaming glasses, had thrown off their habitual reserve hand permitted themselves unseemly jokes, indecent allusions, and lascivious antics.

Odette Myosotis, not to be left out in the cold, exaggerated things, and abandoned herself to the embraces of anyone who felt inclined to thrust a hand into the warm, perfumed recesses of her bodice or found amusement in exploring the mysteries of her sex. She had thus adopted a thoroughly free and easy manner. With her outrageously low dress, now open her waist; her legs bare; she rolled about on the divans, exciting by all sorts of teasing enticement her two neighbours who, at last worked up to frenzy by the wagging of her rosy tongue and the leering glances of her fine eyes, seized her in their arms. The fair bacchante repulsed them, while she laughed hysterically, and the two cocks, now quite in heat, disputed the possession of her undulating body. At last one of the gentlemen had to give way. The other threw himself upon his prey, and by a vigorous movement spread her thighs apart, tearing a pair of short silk drawers violently to clear a passage for his erect, bursting member that he had managed skillfully to extract from his breeches.

Odette was laughing like a madwoman, uttering little shrieks as if afraid, and for the sake of the onlookers, offering obstinate resistance to the efforts of her partner which served to augment his amorous ardour. She ended by giving way, and then there ensued on that divan a Homeric struggle; a bestial, insane parody of ravagement; a roggering bout in which inarticulate cries followed love-bites and voluptuous clinging, clawing embraces, until the moment when nature's sluices opened, and both of them fell back writhing in the final acute spasm of supreme animal enjoyment.

All the spectators had followed the scene with increasing interest. Each man had taken a woman on his knees and the most lascivious caresses were exchanged. Breasts, stripped of their finery, stood up white and firm, their rosy buds stiff with excitement. The naked globes were offered freely to the audacious caresses of the men, to their kisses, and their lustful embraces, without counting those satyr-like wanderings of fevered mouths and lust-hungry hands to unexplored nooks and crannies of the body, that cannot be imagined, nor still less described.

Impassible, the Count and myself looked on. My master, phlegmatic and cold as was his wont, seemed to derive more intense pleasure from the contemplation of this unbridled scene than if he had played a more active part in the battle of venereal fantasy.

As for me, I was, as may be imagined, as excited as possible, but I could allow nothing of it to appear and although I should have liked to have wallowed in my turn in the thick of the fight, rolling on a sofa, tasting divine enjoyment in the arms of my Giovanina, I could not retire without permission from my master.

In one snug nook, Count Popolsky was consoling himself for the infidelity of his beloved Odette by brutally running his hands over every charm of beauteous Liane de Vibrecoeur, who, unmindful apparently that a great, hairy Polish hand had lost itself in the dark path between her plump hinder cheeks, had slipped her bejeweled tapering fingers into his trousers and seemed, by very scientific touching, to provoke most agreeable sensations in her noble aggressor.

Cleo Montauciel had taken upon herself to rouse the spirits of the chief mate, who seemed to experience extreme pleasure in the little game to which the impassioned creature was devoting her energies. On her knees before him, she was ardently worshipping the staff of life that projected itself far out of the nether habiliments of the lusty sailor. Cleo was so awe-struck at its huge proportions that she could not refrain from imprinting a kiss on its ruby head. Too much champagne caused her to miss her aim, no doubt, and that is why, I suppose, half of the mariner's mainmast disappeared down the throat of the enraptured cocotie.

Stella Carina was lying back gasping in the arms of Lord Reginald — and no wonder, for they had adopted a very singular position. She was seated a-straddle on his knees, and seemed to be playing as do little children when they sing, "Ride a cockhorse to Bambury Cross". But on looking more attentively, I could perceive that the noble lord was simply engaged busily and energetically poking his Dulcinea in the position in which they relatively found themselves. This explained to me the ride the languishing girl was taking and which, though certainly original, was perhaps rather fatiguing. It gave her exquisite delight, to judge by her licentious exclamations, galloping movements and swayings of her robust hindquarters.

I followed the phases of this interesting amorous combat until the critical moment manifested itself in rather too evident a manner, for all at once, together with the chair on which they were seated, the naughty couple rolled on to the floor, giving out grunts of voluptuous enjoyment and of passion that was only half satisfied.

One of Lord Seacombe's friends was nursing seductive Renee Danglars, whilst a big, fair-haired fellow was amusing himself in a corner by tickling little Micheline Darcourt in the fragrant bushes of her armpits and down her spine, so as to drive her to a paroxysm of lewd excitement and to still further sharpen if possible their evidently blazing desire.

The two young girls, fuddled with champagne, Tendered wild by exciting and lascivious caresses, abandoned themselves entirely, wriggling about, and seemingly transported with lust.

Their inmost secret sexual feelings were sufficiently exacerbated and they were ripe and ready to give themselves up without reserve to him who would break down the barrier of their physical virginity. But the two gentlemen did not seem at all in a hurry to do so. They appeared to find more tasty pleasure, more piquant pastime, in driving the maidens to the frontiers of insensate, raging desire; forcing them, as it were, to offer themselves and beg of their own free will that their bodies be taken and violated. It almost seemed to me as if these gentlemen wanted to bring the girls to that point, in order then to let them go without satisfying the amorous unreasoning lust they had caused to arise in the poor little dears.

I concentrated all my attention on the two couples. The partner of Renee Danglars, more audacious, bolder than his comrade, had lifted up the petticoats of his charming companion and was gently smacking from the filmy petticoat beneath the Directoire dress Renee was wearing. He had unbuckled the clasps that held up to her shoulders the pretence of a low bodice. The entrancing creature now appeared with the tempting twin glories of her bust entirely bare, abandoning herself to the caresses and soft embraces of her lover, who now and again gently pressed these swelling globes, kissing and nibbling their rosy points. The fellow was not doubt having a good time. He was half undressed, and had contrived to slide into Renee's hand his crimson pego which jerked itself spasmodically. The fair maid was careful not to let go her agressor's member. She uttered tiny, jerky cries, such as: "No! No! I won't! and then began to laugh under the tickling hand of the young man.

Micheline, in the simplicity of her Diana disguise, certainly gave herself up unrestrainedly to her companion's caresses, but I could see that she struggled and resisted the touchings of her lover who had passed his hand beneath her tunic and was endeavouring, while fingering her calves and thighs, to reach as far as the grotto of love. The charming girl barred its road by tightly pressing her dimpled buttocks together, refusing to let him get any nearer to the goal.

I felt sure that her resistance was genuine and that she would not give way. She must have taken fright at the last moment, notwithstanding her natural excitement and intoxicated condition. Like his comrade, the young man had undone his trousers and he tried hard to slip his poker into Micheline's grasp. But she quickly withdrew her pretty plump little fingers as she felt the contact of the stiff, hot, palpitating staff, and I caught in her look a secret terror.

The aspect of that threatening instrument brought her back to reality. Yet she opposed no resistance to her lover while he was greedily sucking her nipples, kissing her ears and eyelids; licking her lips and throat; thrusting his vaggish tongue far into her mouth — in fact, wherever he could put it. She, however, still remained with thighs nervously pressed together, her teeth clenched in mute protest. She victoriously obstructed the efforts of her assailant, energetically and resolutely refusing to let him advance on the road to paradise.

The scene was becoming really interesting.

Next to the saloon was a little cabin which served as a smoking-room, and where there was no one at that moment.

All around us, the guests were laughing, shouting, and rolling on the ground in an immense saturnalia. The scene had changed to a positive orgy. Lord Reginald had told me to look after the orchestration, and I acquitted myself of the mission with the utmost zeal, so that thanks to me, loud music continued without interruption, playing the most lively tunes, whilst the men, maddened by champagne and lust, passed the women from one to the other, and back again.

All around me mad embraces and lascivious caresses were being exchanged. Violent and lustful copulation was going on, but I did not lose sight of the two virgins.

Renee, mad with desire, tremulous with sensual longing, had fallen back upon a divan behind a group of flowering shrubs and, extended on her back, almost nude, her thighs most immodestly outspread, she awaited, panting with impatience, the final supreme attack of her cavalier which would enable her to rank among women.

But her lover, too much excited, or too drunk, leaning over her, his member standing up erect, seemed unable to find the way. In a feverish clasp, Renee drew him to her. He murmured some passionate words of love, stumbled, and got up again, but without succeeding in doing anything. Three or four times the violet-red head of his tool had touched the coral slit of pretty Renee, without being able to penetrate her. She raised herself up in sudden violent jerks, as if to welcome the dagger of which she now eagerly desired the stab. But in vain, the unfortunate man could never succeed, and utterly exhausted, rolled prostrate on the carpet.

Renee, stupefied, as it were, insane with heady wine and unsatiated lust, remained motionless, alone, her thighs still widely apart, her gaze wandering, seeking satisfaction for her overwrought senses, in doing to herself with her finger, what the drunken man had been unable to effect by means of the instrument with which Nature had gratified him for that purpose.

At this juncture, my attention was drawn elsewhere. The resistance opposed by little Micheline to her lover had evidently exasperated him and made his desire rise to an uncontrollable pitch of excitement.

Being strong and vigorous, in a sudden movement, he lifted up in his arms the young girl who, taken by surprise and astonished, could scarce make out what was happening to her.

In less time than it takes me to relate, the ravisher, carrying his victim, had rushed into the little smoking-room, rapidly closing the door behind him and slipping the bolt.

A very small glass window, placed just on one side of the orchestration, and its panes in part hidden by that instrument, permitted only to see into the small room where the young man had just borne his reluctant sweetheart. My place was a good one for observing what took place inside and, as nobody had noticed the disappearance of the couple or else had attached no importance to it, I could quite at my ease and without fear of interruption, follow from beginning to end what was about to be unfolded before my astonished eyes.

I now had the opportunity of assisting at a most exciting and bewilderingly obscene ravagement conducted according to classic rules.

The young satyr, nearly out of his wits, had thrown Micheline on to a divan, where he maintained her solidly, covering her with caresses the while, and showering ardent kisses upon her.

I made out that he was speaking to her and that she replied. He must have been addressing lowing words to her, imploring her to give way to his passion, but she, panting for breath, resisted, and her movements proved to me that she was unwilling to bestow upon him the gift of her jewel of maidenhood. In the combat, the trousers of the rutting male fell down over his reels.

By a sharp kick, he got rid of the garment, and as, intentionally or not, he wore no drawers, he remained simply in his shirt.

During the struggle between the young couple, pretty Micheline had ended by being stripped of most of her garments, for her lover with real frenzy had torn off bit by bit her scanty costume of Diana. Notwithstanding her rebellious endeavours, he had reduced her to a state of absolute nakedness. Her lovely hair, all disheveled, floated loose upon her satin shoulders, rendering their whiteness still more striking.

He was doing all he could to persuade her by word and gesture, but the more he talked, the more she resisted, and I could see him vainly trying to tear asunder her thighs which she kept continually pressed together. Doubtless, she shrieked, but as I did not want to lose sight of a single incident of this striking scene, I set the orchestration at work playing the overture to "Il Trovatore", followed by Wagner's "Walkyrie", thus preventing the slightest sound from reaching beyond the walls of the tiny cabin, and also to smother the noise of what was occurring within.

Micheline, in her distress, plied both arms and legs to try and throw off her companion, who was holding her fast in his passionate embrace.

He almost bruised her in his sturdy arms kissing her madly all over her body, while she, as she stiffened her limbs, caused her heaving breasts to stand out proudly, the red nipples, swollen with kisses, rising up victoriously, calling for more caresses and for the close contact of feverish loving lips and tongue. But the young man, breathless and beside himself, wanted more than this amorous dalliance. As if no longer knowing how to contain himself and lost in lust, he mastered and subjugated her, now and again putting his hands over the mouth of the dear girl who writhed in indescribable disorder as he sought to smother her cries, which I could not hear.

Micheline, evidently exhausted, having no longer any strength left, was plainly weakening.

I could see that much clearly, and in proportion as the resistance of the maiden grew more feeble, so did the ardour of the enterprising youth increase.

I perceived that the lovely girl was on the point of succumbing, and, indeed, buy a sudden and violent movement, her enamoured lover managed to slide one of his knees between Micheline's thighs. She could no longer fight against the pressure and all trembling was obliged to capitulate. Her strength gradually left her.

She still struggled like a demon, but uselessly. Solidly established atop of her, and between her thighs, the young man now vigorously attacked the citadel. By the wild contortions of the poor lassie, by her wriggling and writhing, I could guess that the barrier of her maiden centre of love had been ruthlessly passed. The young fellow now, without stopping, plied his truncheon strongly — he was not hard at work for nothing!

And suddenly, in a last superhuman and truly spasmodic effort, Micheline raised up her body, and then fell back unconscious, after having given one despairing cry. She was no longer a virgin. Her shriek had prevailed over the sound of the orchestration, and everybody rushed to the smoking-room. But the mad mob soon retired when the door was found to be closed.

"Let them alone! I whispered, with a knowing wink. "They love each other too well to be disturbed!"

CHAPTER V

*

Each One In His Turn

I cannot say how the ball ended, for I had retired, leaving the gentlemen to their voluptuous amusements. My readers will understand that all I had witnessed, all the unbridled episodes that had followed in such rapid succession, had contributed not a little to rouse, within me an amount of desire and lustful appetite which I promised myself to largely glut with my little darling — Giovanina.

Free at last and without apprehension, I wended my way towards her cabin, or rather towards mine, for it was there that she had been installed, while I had settled down as well as I could in other quarters.

I tapped at the door, but no response was made. On knocking again, I could hear my little Venus replying to me in her jargon — half French and half Italian.

"Wait a bit, sir! A couple of minutes only, and I will open the door!"

Why did she not open at once? I was still putting that question to myself, when I again hear her voice — this time ringing out clearly, in silvery tones:

"All right! Come in — but in one minute only, I beg of you!"

At the same time, I could hear the bolt being drawn back.

Despite my impatience, I waited two minutes, and then throwing open the door, I advanced boldly within.

I have already had occasion to mention that after the Count had disinterestedly given Giovanina up to me, I purchased for her clothing and underlinen according to my taste.

Guess my amazement when I perceived Giovanina, her hair hanging down. She was stretched upon a small, low divan, and was lightly clad in a gauzy, rose-coloured dressing-room.

It was trimmed with cream ribbons and lace. Besides being half-open, the peignoir, cut very low in front, permitted vague glimpses of the openwork upper part of a white cambric chemise edged with coquettish sky-blue ribbon and bows.

Negligently extended, she reclined swinging her small feet daintily fitted into clinging, white satin slippers, and her slender ankles, encased in black silk stockings, through the fine meshes of which the skin could be seen, pink and tempting, were fully exposed. This contrasted clearly with the lily-white slippers and the tint of her rose wrapper.

Her attitude was so languidly suggestive; the picture before me was so enticing, that I could not do otherwise than glue my lips—to those of the lovely girl, at the same time dropping on my knees in adoration at the foot of the divan.

I began to caress her. I kissed the open space between her youthful breasts, so full of vigour and so dainty to the eye and taste. I lingeringly devoured her voluptuous mouth, and she let me dwell upon her melting, luscious lips.

I slip my hand stealthily under her dressing-gown, intending to caress her slender ankles and elegant calves. Mounting gradually higher, I started, suddenly meeting with naked flesh. I then discovered that Giovanina, by a refinement of coquetry, had put on a pair of my socks.

I cannot tell whether she read my astonishment in my looks, but she spontaneously confessed to me that, stimulated by curiosity, she had witnessed, through the keyhole, a great part of the licentious debauchery in the saloon, and over-excited by what she had seen, had determined to prepare a surprise for me. Knowing that I had taken no active part in the proceedings, she had decked herself to receive me. In her girlish imagination —yet so refined — the sensual child had sought to give more piquancy to our meeting; to render herself more desirable and more seductive. That was the reason for her putting on my socks. They fitted her, as luck would have it, to perfection and made the whiteness of her beautiful skin stand out more conspicuously.

I listened to her, more and more delighted as she innocently unfolded the story of her artless scheme. I could no longer contain myself. I must possess her! In my eyes, she seemed more lovely than all those whom I had just seen was wallowing in the salacious orgy.

But when I wanted to clasp Giovanina in my arms and make her taste supreme delight, I was forced to abate my pretentions. By an inexplicable caprice, she would not let herself be taken and enjoyed. She rebelled, and her resistance served to still further excite my ardour. I begged and prayed; I almost crushed her in my arms. All to no purpose! She still resisted.

What could be the matter with her? Was it woman's whims or any other sentiment? Was it voluptuous refinement? I cannot tell.

But most certainly, I was that night obliged to take her by force in order to possess her.

Reluctantly grasping the stern fact, that I must put forth brute strength, I struggled with her, but of course without hurting her. She told me plainly that she would not have me. I was embarrassed by my clothing, so that, all in a fever, I left her to herself and was quickly undressed.

Quite naked, without a vestige of clothing or underwear to impede my movements, I returned to the attack, more maddened with the most acute desire than ever before in my life.

She had watched me tearing off my garments, following my movements with looks as if to provoke me, an undefinable smile on her lips and, when I approached her., she said to me passionately, in panting accents:

"Oh, come! Come then! Try your hardest! You shall not have me! I won't let you get into me! You shan't enjoy me!"

She drove me crazy, and like a stallion in heat, I threw myself upon her. Her half-opened peignoir surrendered to my ardent kisses her voluptuously tempting breasts. Through the fine cambric of her chemise, I could lengthily breathe the intoxicating, flagrant emanations of her moist flesh, palpitating beneath the pressure of my feverish, trembling fingers. I hardly remember what I did in my state of mad desire — but certainly many wildly fantastical acts of loving lewdness.

After an indescribable wrestling combat, during which we both of us rolled upon the softly carpeted floor, I contrived to take up my position between her thighs. Seizing firm hold of her two sturdy, hard, plump posterior globes, I drew her to me, ready to pierce her with my dart.

She wriggled about beneath me like a serpent, and by reason of her leaps and sudden bounds, I could not find an opportunity to drive home into her casket of sexual enjoyment the magic rod destined to pierce her and subdue her to my will.

All at once I felt her giving way. She had attained the acme of excitement, and this supreme paroxysm of her womb's delight, at the same time as it induced in her a certain feeling of faintness, also caused her thighs to slightly open. Brief as the moment was, it sufficed for me to get the upper hand, and to lodge in the perfumed bower of love the gardener bound to water it with soothing dew.

As on the day when she lost her virginity, she had the same voluptuous swooning spasm, and fell back in my arms, half dead. She had succumbed a second time.

Why had she acted thus? Was it vice, or some deep lust-thirst, that had incited her to this sweet comedy? Or had unseemly curiosity caused her to seek for sensations hitherto unknown?

It would be difficult for me to answer. I can only say that she was that night most delicious, and adorable. She made me pass some hours of love that will remain uppermost in my memory until I die.

Seeing her now at my mercy, in my power, and finding her so well disposed, I gave her, according to my powers, all the enjoyment I could — but she was well-nigh insatiable.

She lent herself without demur to all my fancies, and even experienced great pleasure, as I could often feel her floodgates of sexual sap freely opening, and the tight folds of her warm sheath throbbing on the colon of my straining shaft. Giovanina let herself be futtered in front, from behind, dog-fashion, kneeling — in fact, in every possible manner; and the more she got, the more she appeared to desire, until at last, exhausted and worn out with fatigue, we fell asleep, locked in each other's arms.

CHAPTER VI

*

The Refinements Of Captain Bullock

The next day, when I turned out and hurried up the companion ladder to breathe the delicious, briny morning air, I found the deck of the *Water-Lily* quite deserted. Sitting by herself, and looking rather dull, was Renee Danglars, pensively leaning over the ship's side-rail, folio-wing with her eyes the yacht's wake in the blue waves, or the magnificent panorama which unfolded itself before us, for we were now entering the Gulf of Messina.

Later on, I learned the cause of pretty Renee's melancholy attitude. She had not yet been able to meet with her admirer, and alone, of all the others, she had been unable to make the acquaintance of the great propagating instrument of the human race — the magic wand that rules the fair sex.

On the other hand, I learned that Micheline had shut herself up in her cabin, while the ravisher of her innocence was enjoying well-earned repose in his comfortable bunk, and still dreaming of her, who, in spite of himself, he had violently deflowered.

It was just past midday when the first passengers showed themselves on deck.

All of them, without exception, appeared to be done up and

exhausted. After the night of orgy, each of them with his fair partner had retired to his cabin where they no doubt had still continued their amusements in private.

I pretended to see nothing, but when the Count appeared on deck in his turn, quite brisk and lively, I thought I remarked something peculiar in his manner.

"You are astonished to see me so late", said he to me, "contrary to my custom? Well, the matter is simple enough. Lord Reginald, too tired to be able to satisfy his pretty friend, passed her over to me to take his place, and, on my word, I think I have not acquitted myself too badly! Anyhow. I certainly do net regret having accepted the task. Only, I must say that she gave me enough to do — the jade! I had plenty of work on my hands, and I can assure you—that she is not to be satisfied with half-rations. It requires a good deal to content her! By the bye, your little Italian wench — what is she doing? She was exquisite last night.."

"Oh, don't talk to me about her!" said I, dolefully, seizing the opportunity. "She is ill — very ill indeed, in fact; and to speak frankly, I am convinced she has the green sickness — poor-blooded, badly nourished, you know, sir. I fancy that I am already experiencing the effects of the little conversation I had with her a day or two ago."

"Not possible I" exclaimed the Count, astounded.

"Well, in that case, I had a deuced good idea to avoid poking my nose into such a wasps' nest!

"Pray accept my heartfelt sympathy, my friend, and — my regrets!"

What I did was rather blackguardly, but "all's fair in love and war," and after all, my plan was successful.

The exclusive possession of pretty Giovanina was now assured to me.

Lord Reginald, still delighted with the success of the previous evening's entertainment, was already setting his wits to work to arrange something new, and, in a secret meeting held by the gentlemen, it was decided to organize, not a fancy dress ball, but a very select soiree of the highest chic.

For this purpose, as the ladies were not all provided with ball-dresses, we stopped a week at Messina, where the most fashionable dressmaker's were put on their mettle to make, according to Lord Seacombe's designs, some very sumptuous frocks for his female guests.

I was very careful not to let my Giovanina go ashore, notwithstanding the desire she had expressed to me to that effect. I was afraid of her making some unlucky stumble, and she was too lovely for me to risk losing her for the sake of Italy's blue sky.

We passed some merry days in this lively spot, and when the time required for making the dresses had expired, we stood out again to sea. I do not deem it necessary to relate the numerous incidents that occurred during this part of our trip.

We were proceeding under canvas, and not, making great progress, so that it was not till the third day after leaving Messina that we arrived off Cape Spartivento, the extreme point of the Italian boot.

By this time, the fellow — travellers had all shaken down well together and mutual good feeling prevailed. Each one had made his choice.

Count Popolsky had become reconciled with his beautiful mistress, or at any rate appeared as if he was. Micheline, after having been, a little sulky towards her impetuous ravisher, had quite easily become resigned and made no more difficulties. Her large, liquid eyes, enhanced by dark half-moons, were a certain proof that she was far from being lazy. Renee Danglars alone had remained inflexible and refused to submit. The night of the fancy dress ball had left on her mind deep disenchantment, and what was worse, her unskillful admirer, too fickle to let himself be caught by the charms of the pretty girl, had easily consoled himself for her abandonment. He had fallen back on little Montauciel, to the great despair of the old American Captain who found himself, like Count X..., in solitude, and perforce a bachelor, so that he had now endeavoured to get into the good graces of refractory Renee Danglars, whose refined tastes led her to look for something better than the Captain — an old, ugly, hairy satyr.

It is true that Renee Danglars had consented, after a thousand hesitations, and in return for the life of luxury that had been premised her, to bid goodbye to her maidenhead. But she inwardly made a vow to sacrifice her virginity on the altar of love, in the arms of a male who would not be too repulsive. She wanted to surround the event with a certain poetical atmosphere, and one can understand that the crabbed face of the aged sea-dog with his shaggy beard was not likely to find favour in her eyes. In fact, it only inspired her with deep disgust. The very thought of being pressed in the arms of this hoary old rascal sent a thrill of horror through her veins.

Consequently, every time that Captain Bullock returned to the charge, she straight-way sent him to the right about, and after being so often rebuffed, the old chap began to get angry, and found this series of icy snubs disheartening. "God damn it!" he swore. "When you've got women round you, it's to make use of'em! If that saucy strip o'cahco continues to play the prude, so much the worse for her! If she won't haul down her flag by fair means; I guess I'll have to fight her foul! I'll use force if needs be, and the well see who'll get the best of it!"

When Captain Bullock had something in his head, he carried out his plan to the letter. I had overhead him making the above threatening statement, and I anticipated some dark little drama, when the same evening, I saw Lord Seacombe, accompanied by Renee, enter the little smoking-room where the rap of Micheline had been accomplished. A friend of the noble host was already. I saw the "wolf on the prowl", and as, in this case, the wolf was Captain Bullock, I had promised myself to be very attentive to what might occur, for I apprehended that something interesting was about to happen. A ravenous beast of prey was seeking to devour Renee Red Riding-Hood.

Everyone was on deck; the ladies, lazily swinging in hammocks; the gentlemen, reclining in deck chairs, puffing skywards blue spirals of smoke from their cigarettes and pipes.

I had barely time to dissimulate my presence in a dark corner when Captain Bullock passed me. He was quite excited and already slightly fuddled, directing his steps towards the smoking-room, which he entered, slamming the door loudly behind him.

Favoured by circumstances, I rushed into the deserted saloon and hurried to my little observatory of the previous occasion — the small window giving into the smoking-room from behind the orchestration. From there I could follow all that was going on without missing the slightest detail.

I arrived just in time to see the Captain sit down next to Renee. She recoiled from him, which did not prevent the enterprising old lecher from passing his arm round her waist. He then tried to kiss her, but Renee succeeded in withdrawing her lips from the contact of the satyr's whiskey-flavoured mouth. This caused the two gentlemen present, witnesses of the scene, to laugh most heartily.

The Captain's sensuality was evidently ablaze.

I expected that he would proceed to violence, and I was not far wrong.

Renee Danglars was dressed in every-day costume — a white serge skirt and a lace-trimmed white foulard blouse which sloped indiscreetly at the neck, disclosing a white and firm throat.

Her slender figure was moulded in a very close-fitting dark-blue, saucy yachting jacket, enhancing her irreproachable form, more particularly her undulating hips and sturdy posterior charms.

Captain Bullock, by a sudden unexpected assault, upset Renee on to the divan where they were both seated. He had managed, I scarcely know how, to unfasten his trousers which had now fallen down about his heels, and he was able to commence the attack.

Lord Seacombe and his friend, very cool and smiling, seemed to be quite disinterested onlookers. The struggle went on before their eyes, and they followed it with almost indifferent glances.

Renee fought like the very devil. She worked her thighs and her knees with the energy of despair. Her tiny feet, in low tant shoes with high heels, beat the air, and from time to time managed to land a sharp kick on her aggressor's shins.

The lovely legs of the charming girl, encased in brown silk openwork stockings to match her shoes, exhibited their beauty proudly to the view of the spectators of the scene. Her legs, beautifully moulded, thus to be seen as far as the thighs, where rose-coloured silk suspenders contrasted distinctly with the maroon hose, appeared delicate, but full of energy in the resistance opposed to the efforts of the would-be ravisher.

Renee, dressed with taste, disappeared in the mazes of her petticoat and shirts, which, in the struggle, the Captain had tossed over her head. I could only see her thighs moving by sudden jerks and contortions, and which one could guess, beneath the fine material of hex drawers, to be firm and voluptuous. Under the filmy linen, I seemed to see the superhuman opposition she was putting forth to ward off the profaning touches of the Captain seeking with brutal hands to separate the young girl's thighs. He only managed now and again, at rare, intervals, to open her legs — just far enough to permit a glance to be taken of the mons veneris, on which flourished in wild profusion a forest of wanton hairs.

Renee, no doubt, shrieked loudly; but her cries were probably stifled in her skirts, or did not reach my ears.

As the struggle seemed likely to continue indefinitely without the Captain obtaining any other advantage than that of having able for a brief moment to lay his fingers upon his unwilling captive's pussy, Lord Seacombe interfered, saying in a loud and slightly irritated voice:

"Let her go! We shall have her by other means. Sooner or later, she'll be forced to give way!"

As soon as she felt herself free, Renee, at one bound, was on her feet, red in the face, all dishevelled, her bodice undone. She feverishly adjusted her ruffled plumage.

"No matter who — anyone but you!" she shouted, in accents rendered hoarse by rage. "Understand me well! No matter who! I'll give myself up if it must be so, but you, odious Captain Bullock, shall never have me!"

"Shuff and nonsense! panted the elderly libertine, his mouth distorted by a grin of disappointed lust and rage that sought to be a laugh. "Mark my words, you wild-cat — who knows how to play a waiting game, is sure to win at the finish!"

CHAPTER VII

*

An Agreeable Intermezzo

I was far from having an idea of what was about to take place. During the two following days, and which preceded the grand soiree announced by Lord Reginald, a little adventure happened. I was the hero, and it furnished me with a pleasant remembrance that has remained indelibly engraved in my memory, although when I evoke it, I cannot help a sad feeling of regret, as I recollect that the heroine of this episode is for ever withdrawn from the joys of this world. The sequel will show us how.

I had not lost my time with pretty Giovanina who was decidedly growing more seductive every day. She had become really attached to me, and like a wild gazelle, refused to quit her cabin, for fear of anything happening to her similar to what she had been enabled to witness on the night of the ball.

Lord Seacombe, faithful to his promise, had put a roll of twenty-five thousand-franc notes into my darling's hands, merely asking in return a kiss on Giovanina's tempting mouth, which the lovely child gave him, but only after a look that sought my permission.

A thousand pounds sterling were well worth a moist kiss, and although that sum of money was for the nobleman no more than a drop of water in a vast lake, I considered that such osculation was quite sufficient, the more so as the meeting of two tongues very often leads to something else.

That evening I was leaning over the ship's side, gazing at the stars, all alone on the poop of the *Water-Lily*, when I heard next to me the rustle of a silk skirts. Turning round, I found myself face to face with Renee Danglars.

Big tears were rolling down her cheeks from her large, fascinating eyes.

I have never seen a woman weeping without being moved. Unfortunate Renee was therefore all the more interesting to me.

"What is the matter, mademoiselle?" I asked her. "What great sorrow is weighing on your heart?"

She looked at me for an instant full in the face, as if to try and read my inmost thoughts. She them came nearer and leant on the bulwarks close to me, without saying a word, weeping silently as she stared at the waves.

"Come, come!" said I. "Don't take your troubles so to heart — whatever they may be. What is it all about? What grief is consuming you? Is it indiscreet to ask?"

"You are a Frenchman — are you not?" she said. "You are not the same as these Englishmen and Americans, so cruel and so cold. Oh, that I were far from here! Only fancy — but I dare not tell!"

"Say it right out, nevertheless. Don't be afraid. Unburden yourself without restraint."

She hesitated for a moment, and then she admitted to me having been once more exposed on the part of Captain Bullock to a brutal attempt at ravagement from which she had again emerged victoriously, albeit rather brutally handled. I cannot say how it came about, but in the course of our conversation, I was led to confess that I had accidentally been a witness of the scene in the smoking — room. For a moment she was quite confused, and then, as if she had come to a resolution, she said, without looking at me, and gazing fixedly at the sea:

"Is there then for me no means of escaping from this false position?"

I remained silent, without giving an answer. "You do not reply?" She added, after a pause. "You say nothing? Am I then absolutely sacrificed?"

I could not yet reply, but she read my thoughts in my eyes.

Taking courage all at once, she said to me, without a moment's stoppage, but with her head bowed down and her eyelids half closed:

"Listen to me! You are a Frenchman. We are alone! I find myself driven into a dilemma from which I cannot extricate myself. I shall have to succumb in the long run. Yes, I am being punished where I have sinned. I must go through with it to the bitter end. But speaking frankly, I cannot reconcile myself to the idea of being possessed by that old satyr. I had dreamt of something different. I must certainly submit to the inevitable.... and it my own thoughtlessness that condemns me, well then, I am resigned! But never — no, never! — will, I give up my body to Captain Bullock whom I abhor and hate!"

"Shall I tell you?" She continued, after remaining silent for a moment. "I dare not! No, really, I dare not!"

"Never mind! Speak out!" I insisted.

She appeared to resign herself, and coming closer to me, she whispered in my ear, so close that I could feel her curls tickling my cheek — a contact that caused a tremor to run though my frame:

"I don't know what to do, you see. I feel that I must fall sooner or Later. Well then — I prefer to; give myself freely! I dare not offer to myself to you — but — if you like — well! — take me!"

It was now my turn to look her straight in the face. She did not speak a word, but she turned and met my gaze steadily, as if nerving herself to sustain and brave my startled, searching glances.

The temptation was too great. I had before me a beautiful girl, nineteen years old, in the full bloom of her youth, offering herself to my caresses, so as to escape those of an older man who filled her with disgust.

Without another word, I took her round the waist. I drew her to me, and on her trembling lips I imprinted a burning kiss. Then I led her away.

She allowed herself to be helped along like a lamb to the shambles.

We passed unnoticed to my cabin, and I hastened to close the door after us. Then I found myself in presence of the lovely lass — alone with her — who was voluntarily giving herself to me; who had of her own free will made the offer. The situation was for me altogether a new one, and certainly not devoid of charm.

She abandoned herself resignedly. I pressed her to me, kissing her downcast eyelids and her voluptuous mouth; passing my lips over the silky curls playing about her white neck and rosy ears.

Falling back on a divan, I drew her on my knees and contemplated her for a few instants. She gave herself up passively, with closed eyes, but through her long lashes her tears filtered — big, liquid pearls. I thought of the sacrifice of Iphigenia, and for one second felt remorse.

But my scruples soon faded away, when I called to mind the features of the old Captain. If she must undergo the sex-initiation, it were better that she should for the first time swoon from pleasure in my arms than in those of another.

With burning lips, I sucked the salt tears from her flushed cheeks. She nestled obediently in my arms, and, one by one, I freed her from her various articles of dress — her bodice and stays, to begin with. My fingers trembled at the contract of her delicate and velvety skin, which under my touch, I felt was moist, warm and quivering. And that put me all in a fever!

Inert, Renee submitted to my will, without any resistance. She abandoned herself to my caresses. I felt quite dazed and confused. But my sensual excitement was only the more increased.

Beneath the delicate lace trimming of her cambric chemise, her breasts swelled out, heaving with emotions, and stood up temptingly, while their rosy points, like ripe raspberries, almost caused the fine linen to give way under their active pressure.

I had removed her blouse — her beautiful, plump and dimpled arms that I made her put round nay neck, gave me another voluptuous thrill. In her low corset, her exuberant breasts, under the satin and lace; her sculptural shoulders, rendered her desirable and irresistible in the highest degree. I covered her with kisses, to which she did not seem insensible. Still keeping her on my knees, panting and beside myself, so much had the abandonment of her virgin body excited my senses, I undid her tiny shoes and drew off her white silk stockings, that she had fancied to wear that day. Then, no longer able to restrain myself, I finished undressing her and carried her to my couch. It was not difficult for me to lift her chemise and open her drawers, and the mere contact of my fingers with the silk and lace of these mysterious articles of underwear set my blood on fire. I had denuded her down to her chemise. I could see her beautiful thighs, so firm and white, and had pressed my burning lips upon them. She had continued to submit without manifesting the least emotion.

Her passivity began to tire me — I had even allowed my hands to explore the secret regions between her thighs which did not oppose my indiscreet investigations.

"Are you made of marble?" I asked her, feeling myself incapable of enduring her silent resignation. "Do you then feel nothing? Look here, I prefer not to have you! I won't have you — I refuse to make you a real woman, if you care no more than this for what I am doing!"

Her sole reply was to draw me to her. She seized my head in her hands, kissed my lips, and then said in a murmuring whisper:

"Undress!"

I clasped her in my arms, and leaving her for a moment, I took off all my clothes, down to my shirt, and then came back to her, reclining on my bed awaiting me.

Pressed by my impatience, I was about to commence at once my attack on the fortress which it was no longer necessary for me to besiege, and without flattering myself, I was well prepared to come out with flying colours, when contrary to my expectations, Renee gently pushed me on one side, as she whispered faintly:

"Not yet! Not like that just yet! Oh, come — do! No, not yet!"

Until that moment, by a supreme effort of her will, she had restrained herself, but she no longer had the strength to resist the agitation of her senses now at boiling point and, as she was not carved out of stone, she submitted to Nature's laws and gave free course to her feelings. In her turn, she clasped me in her arms, reciprocated my caresses, and was even bold enough to put her hand down — from curiosity probably — as far as my organ of generation. On touching it, she gave a little start which I perceived quite distinctly, but she said nothing.

What appears to me now very foolish and unreasonable is the fact that only a few broken utterances and indistinct words were exchanged between us.

At last, by mutual consent, we prepared to fully consummate the carnal act.

"What must I do?" she murmured coyly.

"Come, darling!" I rejoined.

For one moment, she experienced a sudden upheaval of recoiling rebellion, but with gentle words and soothing caresses and kisses, I persuaded her to let me do as I chose with her. So she submitted to the supreme embrace of the sexes.

Quite exhausted, almost fainting, after I had plucked the flower of her maidenhood and ejaculated freely within her throbbing cleft, she had a slight fit of hysterics. Then she regained her senses and began to cry bitterly. I tried to pacify and console her, and she laughed through her tears.

When I returned to the charge, she gave herself willingly, with all her heart and soul, joyously, and without manifesting the slightest opposition to my desires, as if she felt the necessity of calming her over-wrought nerves by total abandonment to the shower of virile elixir bringing peace to her womb, and quieting her racked brain.

CHAPTER VIII

*

The Gentlemen Enjoy Themselves

When I left my pretty Renee, having conducted her to her cabin, in a state of mind which required composure and rest, I had not the courage to go and see Giovanina who I knew was waiting for me.

I returned to my cabin and was about to enjoy well-earned repose, when I heard somebody scratching at the door. Without apprehending anything, and in rather a bad humour at being disturbed, I found myself, to my conversation, face to face with my lovely Italian mistress, who appeared like an avenging goddess.

The little roguish damsel not seeing me come to her as usual had been waiting for me in vain.

So she enacted a terrible scene of loving jealousy of which I should never have supposed her capable. She had been listening a the door! I sought to pacify her, but could only succeed by employing the supreme argument, and by giving her what she was longing for: the possession of myself. Fearing to lose me, she wanted to gain me back again, and the sly puss set about it so cleverly, with so much skill; so endearingly, I may say, that she made me forget Renee, writhing in my arms, under the caressing perforation of my deflowering member. Greedy Giovanina soon rendered it impossible for me to do any more.

I was forced to quit the arms of my ardent companion in obedience to an imperious summons from the Count, who sent to require my services. It was the date fixed for the grand soiree that had been announced.

I was pretty well occupied all day long superintending the preparations.

I pass over the minor details. It only remains now for me to relate the most astounding and impressive adventure that ever occurred to me in my life.

The evening of the ball, the saloon was brilliantly lighted, and magnificently decorated with artificial flowers. The entire company was assembled; the gentlemen in evening dress and the ladies in magnificent brand-new toilettes, of which I will try to briefly give a faint idea.

Liane d"Vibrecoeur wore a splendid ball-dress of black moire, garnished with white-ribbons from top to toe, even to her low dancing shoes and silk stockings. Her queenly head was surmounted by a splendid aigrette of ostrich feathers and diamonds. H"r bodice was a mere pretence — so low cut was it; and her closely — fit —-ting skirts moulded her tempting thighs and posteriors.

Stella Carina, in a mauve frock, was very elegant and seductive. Cleo Montauciel looked lasciviously lovely and tempting, her beautiful bare arms encircled by thin gold bangles. Blanche de Noirmont and Esther Hazy were dressed alike, in sisterly fashion, robed in elegant princesse costumes of black velvet, with long trains, their sole ornaments being a cream-coloured velvet ribbon fastened with a diamond clasp round each of their white, full necks; their feet being fitted in black satin shoes, and their legs encased in black silk openwork stockings.

Renee Danglars and Micheline Darcourt had chosen — the former, pale blue; the latter, pink. Their outrageously decollete vapoury ball-dresses were of cloudy chiffon muslin trimmed with ribbons and lace. The two young fairies were intensely alluring.

But charming Odette established another record. Sure of her beauty, she realised a positive marvel of skill by appearing in a dress so refined in every respect that it did not admit the possibility of the least of her charms remaining unappreciated. She had displayed such science in the arrangement of her costume that she might have turned the heads of all the men, even had she been less pretty. She was irresistibly tempting from head to foot, and from the moment of her entrance was surrounded by the gloating rakes.

There was plenty of dancing, and it seemed as if all was likely to pass off in a proper manner, within the bounds of an evening party of good society. Suddenly, at a sign from Lord Reginald, the dancers stopped, and the music ceased.

When everybody was gathered round their host, the latter raised his voice.

"Ladies and gentlemen", he announced, "I am obliged to bring to your notice a grave complaint which has been made against a person who I will not mention for the moment. As it is a matter which must be settled once for all, and would otherwise tend to disturb the previous perfect harmony existing among us, I propose that complainant and defendant be heard contradictorily, upon which we shall be able in full knowledge of the case to decide what punishment is to be inflicted on the delinquent. We will therefore constitute a tribunal, which I reserve myself the right of presiding as judge, and I invite Count Popolsky and three other gentlemen to assist me members of the court."

As may well be supposed, this speech was not without causing great astonishment. No one knew what the case was about and the guests mutely interrogated each other with enquiring glances. But all doubts were soon set at rest, when it was found that Captain Bullock was the plaintiff, and little Renee Danglars, the alleged culprit.

The Captain bluntly exposed his grievances, complaining bitterly of the scornful conduct of the pretty girl who had repeatedly repulsed his advances. This he took to be an insult. Such an awful affront called for satisfaction, his feelings having thus been deeply wounded, and his manly dignity turned into ridicule.

Renee, who had become the cynosure of all eyes, sat bolt upright alone in a corner of the saloon. She hardly knew whether to take this matter seriously, or in a comic vein. Ought she to laugh or to cry? When asked what she had to say in her defence, she advanced smiling to the middle of the room and replied to the questions put to her by Lord Seacombe who, with imperturbable serenity, played the part of the president of a law-court. His examination did not last long.

"Mademoiselle", began Judge Seacombe, "you have just head Captain Bullock's complaint. What foundation is there for his reproaches? Have you really, as he affirms, repelled his gallant advances, and if so, why?"

"My answer is simple enough", replied Renee, still smiling. "It is true that I rejected the Captain's amorous offers. That I admit, unreservedly. As for my motives, gentlemen, you eyes must show them to you. Just look at that old buffer's frontispiece! Did your ever see a more ugly mug? No, there, frankly — do you really think that I could lie down with such an old beast? Do you fancy honestly for one single moment that a dismal conjunction of that kind could cause me any pleasure?"

"Pleasure or no, mademoiselle, that is not the question. It is not the duty of the court to enter into details of your unreasoning likes and dislikes. You could not expect the Captain to be the only one on board to be thrust out in the cold when all the rest of us are having plenty of — ahem! — poking. When you agreed to come with us, you knew well enough that it was not to gaze at the stars, but that our intention was to amuse ourselves, madly — to satiety. Now, it appears to me, that on the night of our fancy dress ball, you were not quite so coy, and I cannot admit that you should now play the prude with our good friend Captain Bullock. We are on this earth to enjoy ourselves; to revel in love's delights, and women are made for love. You are intelligent, my dear, and quite willing to profit by all the advantages of your present situation. You are quite ready to amuse yourself on this pleasure trip; to laugh and sing; put on pretty dresses, and wear jewels — our frank gifts. But when in return, you are asked for a mere bagatelle; just the trifle of a few minutes of fleshly abandonment, you refuse."

A certain feeling of uneasiness began to take possession of Renee, who saw that the reproaches addressed to her were seriously meant. Therefore she added:

"But I never refused. All I say is that I will not have connection with the Captain. No matter with whom, rather than with him — with you, if you like?"

"You ought to have arranged matters better when we all started together. You were assigned by lot to the Captain. His complaint is justified, and you must submit. The order of the court — and my fellow judges concur — is that you beg Captain Bullock's pardon, and surrender yourself to his desires — to all his desires! Do you understand, mademoiselle?"

"Never!" exclaimed Renee, stepping resolutely forward. "I shall never belong to that man!"

"Is that your last word?" asked Lord Reginald.

"Yes, Lord Seacombe — my very last word!" replied Renee, in a savage tone seating herself next to Micheline.

"Very good, mademoiselle", rejoined his lordship. "The case has been heard, the judges will now deliberate on their verdict."

The "court" retired into the smoking-room for about twenty minutes, during which time, the company chatted and laughed.

Odette, speaking to Renee, whom Micheline had already endeavoured to render no submissive, said to her:

"Why don't you give in, you stupid! Get into bed with Bullock! Go on and let him have you! What harm can it do you? Do you suppose that his tool is not so good a one as anyone else's? I've no patience with such a stubborn child! If you only knew! It's always the same after the first time a girl's been poked!"

"Fiddlesticks!" said Renee, casting a furtive glance at me. "You may so, but I don't think it can be the same with every man! After all, if you must know my ideas on the subject, the old fellow sickens and disgusts me — there!"

"Well, my girl," replied Odette, "I don't wish you any harm, but you'll see what'll happen. The Captain has taken a fancy to you. He'll have you at no matter what cost, and I greatly fear that you will be obliged to give him your maidenhead! A scene of ravagement! That will be rare fun!"

"I should like to see it, indeed!" exclaimed Renee, with fire in her eye, and clenching two baby fists.

At this moment, the gentlemen-judges returned to the saloon, after having, it was said, examined the grave affair in all its bearings, and I must admit that nobody had the least idea of what was now about to occur.

In clear and ringing accents, Lord Reginald at once communicated the decision of the "tribunal ":

"We have unanimously recognised that Mademoiselle Renee's

conduct deserved exemplary punishment and it shall be inflicted, even if at the last moment she should consent to what was demanded of her. This is therefore what we have decided by common consent. That Mademoiselle Renee, having behaved like a naughty and capricious child, shall be treated like a whimsical little girl who refuses to obey her elders. She shall have her bottom well whipped and each member of the company here assembled shall give her three strokes with a birch on her naked backside. That will teach her to be capricious!.."

Renee could not believe her ears; she was petrified, stunned. At this juncture, Captain Bullock, taking advantage of the opportunity offered to him, advanced towards her, and seizing her suddenly in his vigorous grasp, prevented her from using her arms in defence.

During this, Lord Seacombe had left the saloon, returning almost immediately with his valet. Tom, a big, strong negro. He must have been no novice at the flogging game, for he seemed at Renee to realise what was required of him. Seeing Renee struggling like the very devil in the arms of Captain Bullock, from whose clutch the frightened girl was trying to escape.

Tom simply asked:

"Is that her?"

Lord Reginald made an affirmative sign.

Tom at once advanced towards Renee and placing himself before her, he seized hold of her slender wrists and then said to the Captain:

"Let go, sah!

Bullock stretched his hands apart, and Tom, by a surprise movement, having passed Rene's arms over his shoulders, lifted her up on his back where she remained suspended. In vain she kicked and struggled. The black servant held tight.

One of the gentlemen seized her left ankle; another clutched the right, and she was thus reduced to immobility on the broad back of her tormentor.

Lord Reginald then came forward, lifted up Renee's skirts and petticoat and threw them over her head.

Her rich and elegant underclothing thus exposed to view, the sight of her hidden charms was eminently soul-stirring. It was of a nature to trouble the senses and raise voluptuous ideas among the spectators.

It was still worse when Lord Seacombe, speaking to the Captain, said:

"It is now your turn! You have been insulted, so you must begin by undressing the prisoner!"

The Captain did not wait to be told twice. He drew near Renee, and passing his right hand in the slit of her drawers, he gently slapped her buttocks. Then for a moment his rough fingers disappeared between her thighs. Renee howled and endeavoured though uselessly to resist. She was held as in a vice and all her efforts served but to make the male guests laugh.

With skill and dexterity such as I should never have supposed Captain Bullock to possess, he undid the young girl's drawers, letting them fall down to her heels. Two splendid posterior globes were exposed to view. It was enough to send a tremor of lust through the most indifferent man.

I do not know where they came from, but there suddenly appeared a dozen birch rods coquettishly tired up with differently coloured ribbons.

The Captain was the first to begin.

Weighing his strength, with a well calculated stroke, he aimed the initial blow at Renee's lovely hemispheres.

The young girl gave a violent plunge and uttered a shrieking cry of agony which pained me to the heart, and I could read in the eyes of the other women an immense feeling of pity.

A second and a third blow applied with still greater vigour produced two opposite effects. Whilst unfortunate Renee was writhing with her whole body trembling with pain and shame, and shaken by internal sobs, it seemed to me that the witnesses of the flogging tragedy were gradually being overwhelmed by peculiar excitement, betraying itself in their staring eyes, and in the tremor of their lips. They appeared to feel a certain strange and hitherto unknown sensuous enjoyment which I confess was also gaining me.

After Captain Bullock, it was the turn of Lord Reginald. He approached and probably finding the exposed surface too limited for his purpose, threw up the poor victim's entire chemise right over her head.

Then with a certain degree of deliberate calmness and without any haste, he applied his three strokes, which hat the same effect as those given by the Captain, with this difference, however, that they drew more doleful complaints and still more painful cries from the unhappy martyr.

I cannot say what whim or caprice seized his brain, but the fact is that after his allotted share of the birching task. Lord Seacombe called to me.

"Come now", he said, laughing, "you can't expect to get out of this! You must take your part in the whipping of rebellions Renee. Give us a sample of Parisian skill!"

I advanced mechanically, and took, the birch that was handed me. I went close to Renee. I could not bring myself to strike her. At the sight of her lovely body, and of her satin skin, already streaked with long ruby, blistered lines, beneath which young, ardent, healthy blood was boiling, I could not retrain myself, but stooping down, instead of beating the bruised flesh with the awful instrument of torture. I imprinted a long and passionate kiss on the part which had been most sorely hurt. My lips were loath to leave Renee's burning, quivering, voluptuous flesh.

My pitying proceeding was looked upon as a stroke of Gallic humour and gallant attention, causing a murmur of applause to salute my retreat. But no one except Renee could understand the meaning of my caress or grasp its real meaning.

The poor child — alas! — had not reached the end of her fearful ordeal. Count Popolsky now took the birch in hand and with a kind of frenzied rage, began to strike in his turn.

Renee gave a cry of intense agony followed immediately by a savage howl.

At the same moment, the negro let go his victim, who fell on the floor. With one bound, she was again on her feet and took refuse in a corner of the saloon where she barricaded herself behind a sofa, like a hunted animal tracked by a pack of hounds. All the women were seized with profound emotion.

After the first moment of surprise, the gentlemen had hastened to gather round dusky Tom, whose neck was bleeding profusely. With a violent bite of her teeth, Renee had torn a piece of sable flesh from Tom's nape. The pain caused him to loose his hold, and he yelled, swore, and jumped about like a demon.

Lord Reginald, in a fury, shared by all his friends on seeing the entertainment brought to so sudden a termination, made a sign to his guests, who all at once surrounded the poor lassie with whom they engaged a furious tussle. Naturally, she was not strong enough to resist their combined attack and was obliged to succumb. Foaming with rage, writhing in the grip of her captors, who now held her down on the floor, she was stripped of her clothing, bit by bit.

This proceeding took some little time. At each fragment of flesh revealed, the men's ardour redoubled and soon amounted to blind, bestial rage. At last, having had everything torn from her with the exception of her chemise, she contrived by a supreme effort to free her quivering body, and got on her feet for a moment. Seized again, the last veil was ripped from her white frame and she now appeared to the gaze of all stark naked and blushing, in all the bloom of her sculptural charms.

It was enough to damn a saint. In the middle of the saloon stood a column supporting the ceiling. This pillar was garnished with red velvet and half fainting, the young girl was bound to it. At blue scarf was wound round her neck, while her hands and ankles were fastened to the column by a silken cord of the same colour which had formed part of her costume.

And now commenced a most sickening scene.

All the spectators, armed with birches, began to thrash the young girl most unmercifully. She gave vent to dismal, heartrending groans.

At last, when they could continue no longer, Lord Reginald, gave a signal and Renee was released. She fell down at full length on the carpet, exhausted by pain and anguish; her dilated eyes conveying an expression of undefinable terror.

Captain Bullock, like a stallion in heat, his gaze being fixed and glassy as of a man demented, in a paroxysm of lust, had rapidly torn open his trousers and thrown himself upon his prey.

She had not the slightest strength left and offered the merest shadow of resistance.

She merely made a few convulsive starts when the Captain, clawing at her poor, bruised body, upon which could be seen drops of blood crimsoning his brutal fingers, clasped her in a bear-like hug, and possessed her — roughly, vilely, fully. The poor child gave one pitiful moan and then fainted, while on his part, the grunting brute, like a drunken man, satiated his beastly fornicating lust, beneath the excited gaze of the spectators who, breathless and in a state impossible to describe, followed every phase of this dramatic episode.

Renee, half dead, was enveloped in a dressing-gown and carried to her cabin, where she was left to the care of a lady's maid who thought the whole affair was quite natural. The serving-maid merely shrugged her shoulders when she saw the wounds inflicted on the unfortunate young woman's bottom.

CHAPTER IX

*

"L'appetit vient en mangeant"

But this was not to be the last of our surprises on that eventful evening. Appetites excited by the little scene of flagellation that had just been enacted, and which might have satiated many, Lord Seacombe and his friends proposed not to stop there. Our host jokingly expressed his opinion, serious at bottom, that being so well disposed they might as well continue the game and give the other ladies, one and all, a slight taste of flogging joys and smarting diversion.

"To punish them for their past and future sins", the merry nobleman summed up.

The gentlemen received this proposal with enthusiasm. But on the side of the ladies, there was a unanimous cry of protestation.

Several among then endeavoured to escape, but this had been foreseen. Precautions had been taken, and the would-be fugitives found the door solidly secured from the outside.

These pretty dames who had just witnessed with a certain amount of enjoyment the fustigation of Renee, by no means expected to be called upon to furnish amusement in their turn, and did not care the least in the world to do so. They demurred vehemently, crying out loudly, shedding tears and declaring that they would rebel. Lord Seacombe inflexible, went and gave two knocks on the panels of the door. It opened, and in walked six sturdy seamen, with decided faces and rough hands.

"Ladies", said Lord Reginald, "let us talk reasonably. You can see that all resistance is useless, and did not serve much in Renee's case. You must admit that for your venial sins you deserve some slight correction. Receive it therefore graciously. It will be so very pleasant for us to cause you a little pain, and give a dash of bitter flavour to the joys we procure you. We shall but love you all the more afterwards, and besides, as we are also not without faults, I promise you in my name and in that of my friends here that we shall gaily, meekly submit to be well whipped in our turn by you, and shall be glad to grant you your revenge."

Count Popolsky and my employer made wry faces at this proportion, but all the Englishmen approved by a nod.

"Please now, darlings", continued Lord Seacombe, "undress your dear little selves. We shall do the same so as not to keep you waiting too long for your revenge. If you refuse, my men here will undertake to serve as your maids."

The first to reply was Liane de Vibrecoeur. She declared that all this threatening fuss was needless. She preferred death rather than such indignity and degradation.

"Very good!" said Lord Seacombe. "We shall see!"

He waved his hand and four men seized the poor damsel. In spite of her desperate efforts to free herself from their brutal grasp, they carried her to a divan, and the two other manners began with their awkward fingers to undress her, commencing with her shoes and stockings.

Liane howled with fury. Foaming at the mouth, she writhed like a serpent, vomiting against Lord Reginald her complete vocabulary of foul imprecations.

"Rogues! Cowards! Rascals! Assassins!" and vile epithets followed unceasingly, leaving the gentlemen quite indifferent, whilst the other girls, stupefied with fear, cowered together in a corner of the saloon, like a flock of trembling sheep.

Meanwhile, the grinning Jack Tars continued disrobing Liane. Her shoulders appeared; then her arms, and her breasts palpitating with emotion. The delicate, white skin of the splendid young woman took on rosy tints at the prolonged contact of the sailors' rude, hard hands.

She was stripped to her chemise, the last veil hiding the treasures of beauty with, which kind Nature had gratified her, their plump magnificence and voluptuous shape being divined beneath the cloudy cambric. When her majestic legs, akin to marble; slender ankles, and at moments, the beginning of her thighs appeared, the sailors stopped short and hesitated.

"Her chemise, too! Off with it!" roared Lord Reginald.

Liane de Vibrecoeur, splendid in her conquering loveliness, her eyes closed, had nothing more to hide from the spectators' gaze.

"You see, girlies", continued Lord Seacombe, "all rebellion is futile. You must submit, with good will or by force! To make an example, and to punish Liane for her foolish resistance, I shall administer to stiff-necked Madame, and on my own personal account, a well-deserved correction! Go on my lads, lay her down on her pretty white belly!"

This was done in a twinkling, and without losing a minute, Lord Reginald administered on the rounded buttocks of the fair queen of Parisian gallantry a vigorous birching which made her scream with pain.

Neither her cries nor her supplications succeeded in calming the ardour of Lord Reginald, who did not stop until he judged that the fair delinquent had received enough.

"Let her go!" he then said, and the men released Liane, who weeping silently, sank down on the cushions.

"Well, ladies, what do you think of it?" asked his lordship. "Will you still be stubborn? I swear that each of you shall have her dose of chastisement in turn!"

It was a critical moment, and the fluttering pets were bound to come to a decision, Micheline — poor little girl! — was shedding bitter tears, in terror of the dreaded operation. The other women, in consternation, did not know to what saint they should address their supplications.

Odette, the lovely and divine mistress of Count Popolsky, then summoned up courage, and advanced bravely.

"It's a beastly bore and a horrible shame to be obliged to put up with this! It wouldn't matter so much if it didn't last so long!" she sighed.

"Well, so much the worse!" she added, "What must be, must! So I prefer to undress myself. Only, my little lord, since you and your friends have such queer tastes, you ought to make a concession. It would be very nice on your part if you would not make us wait too long for our revenge. As there is no means of doing otherwise, let's go in for it! But you, boys, take your share also at the same time as ourselves! There will be always that amount of consolation!"

This despairing sally of Odette caused a laugh. Lord Reginald easily persuaded his friends to accept the charming girl's proposal, and it was unanimously accepted, with the exception of Count Popolsky, my protector, and of course, myself, who none of us had any desire to taste the pleasures of fustigation, even if we were to be eternally damned for refusing. — In the ladies' camp there still remained some fleeting thoughts of revolt, but these were soon overcome.

In less than a quarter of an hour, the entire company was reduced to a state of nature, and each of the ladies having received a bundle of birch, and the gentlemen being armed with the same, the flogging festival commenced at a signal given by Lord Reginald who had requested me to set the orchestration going.

It was to the sound of one of Sousa's marches that the dance of the birch began. It would be impossible to describe the orgy that followed. Rods kissed through the air, coming down swishing and outting bare buttocks and thighs. The sinister whistling of the twigs made my flesh creep.

It had been expressly stipulated that the strokes should fall only on posteriors and thighs, but I am inclined to think that in this wild saraband not a few blows may have strayed on arms and shoulders, or even to mysterious portions of the male and female anatomy generally softly caressed, when touched at all.

It was weirdly fantastical to witness this mad lashing chase round the saloon; to see all these naked men and women writhing beneath the glare of the electric lights — lovely, shapely shoulders upon which disheveled locks floated wildly. It was exciting, maddening to hear the cries of pain and rage. It was a savage spectacle also to see the women, giving stroke for stroke, with ferocious rage; trying to hit harder than the males, and quicker. When, after a bewildering pursuit, as if a wave of insensate lust and wild intoxication of the senses had seized upon all the actors in this scene of flagellating ectasy, couples rolled away exhausted and bruised into corners; on to divans and cushions, as if all were overcome with a sudden mad contagious fit of desire and insatiable loving longing.

When I viewed the men, worked up to a pitch of rutting frenzy, cast themselves on their companions and possess them with howls of sensual voluptuousness, I could not stand it any longer, and escaped to join my Giovanina. She had no cause to complain of the influence of the rod.

CHAPTER X

*

The Final Plunge

Little Giovanina was charming that evening.

She compensated me amply for the long expectation which had inflamed my blood. Although I had taken no active part in the flagellating fun, I found myself almost in the same state of mind as that in which were those gentlemen heroes of the rod after the birching bout in which they had cast off all restraint.

Our happiness was destined — alas! — to be soon troubled by an awakening as sudden as it was disagreeable.

In the midst of our amorous dalliance, a terrible crash was heard. We were roused from our wanton sport by cries of distress and despair.

Terrified, we sprang from our couch, and followed by Giovanina. I rushed on deck. My sweetheart was beside herself with fright.

She clung to me, her hair hanging down, her eyes dilated. Giovanina was almost naked, trembling, and still warm from love's caresses.

In a few seconds, I reached the saloon where there electricity was extinguished, and the most frightful disorder reigned in the vast room. It was quite dark, and I stumbled against several prostrate me and women, their bodies still moist from the passionate embraces to which they had been but a moment before abandoning themselves. They had been torn from their delirium of furious, indiscriminate copulation, and the nature of the disturbing alarm was still unknown to them, but its effect upon everyone was crushing.

Suddenly the lamps lit up again, and I found myself in presence of a tableau of boundless debauchery.

In the middle of the saloon, in a state of complete nudity, almost blond drunk, tossing about like a mad animal, was Captain Bullock, wallowing on the naked and inert body of lovely Renee, who was senseless. The Captain, like a wild beast in rut, was ravishing the young woman's body, while Lord Reginald and Count Popolsky were endeavouring to drag the slobbering satyr from his victim, whom he would not let go, contenting himself, with repeating ignoble oaths in a hoarse and hiccuping voice.

The women, in the costume of Eve, were at a loss to know which way to turn. They screamed and pushed one against the other, without having the presence of mind to rush on deck, while each male, dazed with half satisfied lust and fuddled with champagne, looked stupidly at his neighbour, asking:

"What's the matter? What's up? What the deuce is going on, old fellow?"

At this moment, Tom, the negro servant, rushed into the saloon, calling out in his jargon:

"Quick, massa! Hurry up! De ship she berry near done sinking! We've been run into — smashed up by a big liner! Save yerselves! Ebery man for himself and de debbil take de las' poor sinner!"

Then, without waiting, he flew back to the deck.

With lightning rapidity, a thought flashed through my brain. The captain of the *Water-Lily* was below; the chief mat was off duty, sleeping in his bunk; and the second officer, who had charge of the middle watch, had, I knew, got drunk on champagne. There was therefore no competent man to take charge of our ship. Thus it was that a passing steamer had just collided with the yacht.

I thought only of my own safety and of that of poor little Giovanina.

There are moments in a man's life when his strength is increased tenfold.

I clasped in my arms the body of my darling girl, and carried her up the saloon staircase with no more effort than if she had been a child of two years of age. I felt her whole body trembling like a slender poplar branch shaken by the wind. Her large, haggard eyes were directed at me with an imploring look, I seemed to read in their glances that she had confidence in me and looked to me to save her.

In a few bounds, I gained the deck, followed by the panic-stricken crowd of men and women who, howling with rage and terror, mutually hampered each other's movements on the narrow stairway.

Heady, musky odours arose from the mass of human beings wedged together. The perfumed bodies of the harlots emitted penetrating vapours, increased by the warm fragrance emanating from the skin of all these naked debauchees impregnated with the sweat of amorous caresses and passionate moist kisses, that bad tasted every kind of honey in Cupid's store.

Hot effluvia puffed from the staircase, in which were crowded living beings, who, but a few minute before, were all given up to joy and pleasure, glutted with wanton sensuality. They were now struggling with the energy of despair to escape from threatened death.

This lasted for only a second, but in such moments — seconds are like centuries.

On deck, the crew ran hither and thither distracted. With the instinct of preservation, there had been awakened in the souls of the men, most of them brutal by nature, their implacable egotism, which left no room for a spark of generosity or elevated feeling.

They were enwrapped in the idea of their own safety. Unfortunately, the ship's boats, scarcely ever used, were made solidly fast to the davits, and the rusty chains stuck fast in the blocks.

Like demons, the sailors struck with axes upon the corroded chains.

Time was being lost. I have said why the captain of the yacht was not at his post, and Lord Seacombe, out of his wits, and in the most primitive costume, was doing his best to give orders which passed unheeded.

Far away on the horizon, in a cloud of black smoke, the steamer that had run into the yacht, staving in our bows, causing a terrible leak in our hull, was fast disappearing from our view, fleeing from the responsibilities she had incurred, and leaving us to our inevitable doom.

The graceful *Water-Lily* was slowly settling down beneath the waves.

I was overtaken by terrible anguish. I could see no means of salvation, in the midst of this mob of despairing men and women, mad with fear.

At all hazards, I carried away my Giovanina, more dead than alive, to the afterdeck.

It was with much difficulty that I succeeded. But once there, I gave a cry of joy and relief. I caught sight of the nigger valet. Tom, who, taking advantage of the general stampeding panic, was carrying on his robust shoulders a light racing skiff belonging to Lord Seacombe.

Clutching a carpenter's hatchet that was lying close to one of the ports, I rushed at the darkey.

"Tom!" I cried. "You must take me along with you!"

The nigger looked at me with a chuckle, saying in his lingo:

"You go'ell, same as de odder fools! Boat too small for three. Tom, good nig, strong and brave, he save myself. You drown wid white trash!"

"Vile black hound!" I shouted. "You must launch the skiff and let us get in. I will allow you to come with us. But if you hesitate for one single instant, I'll smash your skull, thick as it may be!"

So saying, I raised my axe, ready and resolved to strike.

At the aspect of my weapon, its bright steel giving out a sinister gleam in the darkness, the giant made a backward bound. As quick as he, I seized him by the throat.

"One step more," I yelled, "and you're a dead man!"

Tom did not reply immediately. He gazed at me in a manner which in certain circumstances would have made my blood freeze in my veins.

I am convinced that at this solemn moment he would have coolly murdered me, if he had possessed knife or pistol.

"Come on den, damn you!" he snarled, with sudden resolution. "Lend a hand!"

I helped him to lower the outrigger and I go in first. The negro followed. The shock, caused by his jump into the tiny boat, mad it float a few yards away from the side of the yacht, now rapidly sinking.

"Jump! Leap quickly into the sea!"

I shouted to Giovanina, who had remained on deck.

With an amount of courage which I should never have thought she possessed, the Italian beauty hurled herself unhesitatingly overboard, although she did not know how to swim.

Tom, who had seized the oars, in two strokes brought the rocking boat to where. The young girl had struck the water, and between the two of us we soon hauled her in, but not without difficulty and danger, for the slightest movement threatened to capsize the frail craft. Hardly was the in comparative safety, than Tom shouted:

"Quick, massa — quick! Sit down and pull like hell! We're bound for Davy Joness's locker!"

Without further hesitation, I seized another pair of oars, and seconded the efforts of the negro, who began to row with all his might. His vigorous efforts made the flimsy cockleshell fly though the heavy sea.

I cast a glance behind. We were only just in time.

At the very moment that one of the yacht's boats crowded with people was leaving the side of the sinking vessel, the:*Water-Lily* bowsprit shop up in the air. The water had evidently swamped the yacht's stern cabins. In a few seconds her bows reeled, and then suddenly, with a fearful plunge, Lord Reginald Seacombe's graceful bark disappeared beneath the surging waves.

A terrible cry of distress rose in the night. Voices, with superhuman accents, joined in one supreme invocation; a shriek of combined agony sounded in our ears, filling us with unspeakable dread and horror.

And that was all. On the immense watery plain, there remained nothing more than rolling waves surmounted with white, foaming crests.

The ship's boat, drawn down in the vortex caused by the sinking *Water-Lily*, was lost with all its occupants. Not a vestige remained of the joyous, light-hearted human butterflies, unless perchance their souls hovered above the abyss wherein now reposed their mortal remains, from which they had been so ruthlessly snatched.

Such is destiny! Of all this exuberant youth; of all this feminine beauty; of all this lust of the senses and of the flesh, nothing remained — nothing!

The next morning, we were picked up by an Italian fishing boat, and two days later landed at Taranto, whence — after a few days had elapsed — Giovanina and I parted from the negro and returned to France.

THE END

CPSIA information can be obtained
at www.ICGtesting.com
Printed in the USA
BVHW041455280722
643250BV00003B/128

9 781535 051484